**"You're cute wh**
**Will told Sama**

You're dangerous ~~t~~
thought. Samantha drew in a breath. "I hope
you're not hitting on me again."

"Me? Wouldn't think of it." Will aimed a thumb
at the center of his chest. "I know the rules." He
nudged her lightly. "Not that there are any rules
about you hitting on me."

"We're not going to need any."

His fingers stroked the inside of her wrist. "Want
to bet?"

Figuring it would be a sign of weakness to
pull away, she stated firmly, "I don't gamble
on love—er, sex. And you're not going to change
my mind," she insisted.

"I know you think that."

"Being in Laramie is not going to change my mind."

Serious now, he said quietly, "I know you think
that, too."

Samantha swallowed around the parched feeling
in her throat. "Yet you're convinced otherwise."

Will lightly took her chin between his fingers and
kissed her mouth, ~~confidence~~ radiating from him.
"Some things I just ~~know.~~"

Dear Reader,

A while back, someone asked me if I had ever seen a bumper sticker that summed up my philosophy on life. I hadn't, but if I were going to design one, I think it would read "Life is messy. Don't be afraid of the mess."

That advice is especially on point for Will McCabe and Samantha Holmes. Will suffered through a divorce that left him feeling he wasn't cut out for marriage after all. Samantha had given up on ever living happily-ever-after when tragedy tore her family apart. Both figured as long as they kept all their defenses up, they wouldn't ever be unhappy again. That was, until they met each other.

Will, Samantha and her brother Howard are three people working at cross-purposes. Three people who ended up loving—and helping—each other despite all the odds. Three people who just might become family in the end, along with Howard's bride, Molly, and all of Will's family, and the friends and neighbors from Laramie, Texas, they meet along the way.

I hope you enjoy this latest visit to the fictional town of Laramie, Texas, as much as I did. For information on this and other books, please visit me on the Web at www.cathygillenthacker.com.

Happy reading!

*Cathy Gillen Thacker*

# Cathy Gillen Thacker
## FROM TEXAS, WITH LOVE

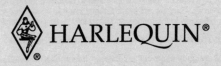

# HARLEQUIN®

TORONTO • NEW YORK • LONDON
AMSTERDAM • PARIS • SYDNEY • HAMBURG
STOCKHOLM • ATHENS • TOKYO • MILAN • MADRID
PRAGUE • WARSAW • BUDAPEST • AUCKLAND

ISBN-13: 978-0-373-75161-7
ISBN-10:      0-373-75161-3

FROM TEXAS, WITH LOVE

Copyright © 2007 by Cathy Gillen Thacker.

This edition published by arrangement with Harlequin Books S.A.

® and TM are trademarks of the publisher. Trademarks indicated with ® are registered in the United States Patent and Trademark Office, the Canadian Trade Marks Office and in other countries.

www.eHarlequin.com

**Printed in U.S.A.**

## ABOUT THE AUTHOR

Cathy Gillen Thacker married her high school sweetheart and hasn't had a dull moment since. Why? you ask. Well, there were three kids, various pets, any number of automobiles, several moves across the country, his and her careers and sundry other experiences (some of which were exciting and some of which weren't). But mostly, there was love and friendship and laughter, and lots of experiences she wouldn't trade for the world.

## Books by Cathy Gillen Thacker

### HARLEQUIN AMERICAN ROMANCE

Don't miss any of our special offers. Write to us at the following address for information on our newest releases.

Harlequin Reader Service
U.S.: 3010 Walden Ave., P.O. Box 1325, Buffalo, NY 14269
Canadian: P.O. Box 609, Fort Erie, Ont. L2A 5X3

# Chapter One

Will McCabe had known retrieving Samantha Holmes by "whatever means necessary" was not going to be easy. He had been forewarned about the twenty-nine-year-old woman's stubbornness and feisty nature. However, he hadn't expected to have to pull her out of a war zone. But as he left the limo idling at the curb in one of New York City's more questionable neighborhoods, and found his way up the steep wooden steps to apartment 5E, a pitched battle was exactly what it sounded like.

"Okay, that's it!" a female voice shrieked from the other side of the door. The words were followed by heavy footsteps and a karate-style yell. "You ugly looking son of a rodent! I've had it with you making my life so darn miserable!" she shouted over a loud crash and resounding whack that even had Will jumping. "If you won't get out on your own volition, then I'm just going to have to kill you myself!"

Will's eyes widened at the blatant threat.

Howard Holmes had said his baby sister had bad taste in men, but letting a domestic dispute deteriorate to this level of violence was downright foolish. Determined to get her out of there before any more harm was done, Will pounded on the door with his fist. "Samantha! Open up!"

"I can't," she shouted back over the sound of glass shattering.

"Seriously..." He tried the door handle and to his frustration found the latch locked. "We need to talk!" He pounded on the door again.

"I don't think so," she retorted.

Will winced when he heard another loud crash. A neighbor from down below quickly opened his door, peered out, then slammed it shut.

"Samantha!" Will ordered. "Open up now!"

The woman inside muttered something he couldn't quite catch. Then she screamed in terror. To heck with waiting, Will thought, as he muttered an oath and kicked the door in. It swung open to reveal a studio apartment that had definitely seen better days.

Samantha Holmes whirled, looking every bit as beautiful in person as in the photos Will had seen. Her delicate face was dominated by long-lashed, dark brown eyes, a straight nose and luscious lips. Thick glossy hair, the color of dark cherrywood, tumbled in loose waves past her shoulders. She came nearly to his chin—which made her about five foot eight—and every inch of her was feminine, from her silky skin to her full breasts, trim hips and long, sexy legs. Eyes flashing, she brandished a broom, while the biggest mouse Will had ever seen raced across the floor.

"Don't just stand there gawking," she commanded, stepping over a pile of broken glass as the skinny gray tail disappeared beneath the sofa. "Shut the darn door and help me catch him!"

Relieved that it hadn't been a man Samantha Holmes was fighting with, Will complied. "You know, they have exterminators for jobs like this," he drawled, trying not to notice how great she looked in the cotton sleep jersey that fell halfway to her knees.

Another resentful glare came his way. "An exterminator would kill him," Samantha protested.

"Not necessarily." Will spied a flashlight on the coffee table. Glad this was one problem he could easily solve, he picked the light up and got down on his knees. He turned it on, illuminating the area beneath the sofa, and quickly located the quivering creature. Figuring "Mickey" wasn't going anywhere anytime soon now that it had found a place to hide, Will sat back on his haunches and looked up at Samantha. He was close enough to inhale the alluring fragrance of lavender clinging to her skin. "Besides," he teased, "you just threatened to do that yourself."

Flashing an apologetic smile, Samantha gestured to a metal cage on the floor of the kitchen. "I didn't mean it." She brought the contraption over to Will and set it down between him and the sofa. Hunkering down beside him, she bent to get a look at the frightened mouse, then gave a little shiver. "I just want him out." She rubbed her arms with her hands. "Preferably right now." Climbing to her feet once again, she added, "I was hoping if I scared him sufficiently he would take off and never return."

Aware he was at eye level with her thighs, Will stood up, too. Then he realized her arms weren't the only part of her that was cold. Resolutely, he pushed away the enticing vision and turned back to the task at hand—capturing the mouse that was currently making Samantha Holmes's life miserable.

Will glanced around, sizing up the threadbare furniture, several wardrobe racks of clothing, well-organized, and an equally impressive tier of shoes and handbags. Obviously, when it came to work attire, Samantha Holmes spared no expense. "How long has your rodent buddy been here?" he asked.

"A week." She gnawed on her lower lip as she looked up at Will. "I've tried everything to capture him so I could take him to the park and set him free." She shrugged. "Cheese. Peanut butter."

Will eyed her kitchen and found it sparsely equipped. "Maybe that trap you set up doesn't look quite so humane to him. Besides—" he nodded at the cereal boxes on the counter, their bottoms eaten out "—why should he settle for a one-course meal when your kitchen cabinets provide a buffet?"

Samantha huffed, the action lifting the luscious curves of her breasts. "You sound like you know a lot about pests," she remarked.

Wishing he hadn't noticed what a great body she had beneath the lavender sleep shirt, and that she wasn't wearing a bra, Will met her eyes. "True, although I try not to live with any."

She made a face. "Very funny," she retorted dryly. Then she narrowed her dark eyes, as if suddenly realizing she shouldn't be trusting him. She tightened her grip on the broom. "Who the heck are you, anyway?"

"Will McCabe," he told her, bracing himself for the worst.

She paused to process that information. "As in the McCabes—of Texas?" she asked finally.

Proud of his family's stellar reputation throughout the Lone Star State and beyond, he nodded. "You got it."

Samantha, however, seemed unimpressed by his lineage. Her scowl deepened. "Owner of McCabe Charter Jet Service in Laramie, Texas?"

Will accepted the credit for all he had accomplished. He angled a thumb at his chest. "That would be me, all right."

"Then I know why you're here and what you want." Samantha glowered at him. "And my answer is no."

"I HAVEN'T ASKED YOU anything yet," Will McCabe stated lazily, his appreciative gaze drifting over her.

Samantha angled her head to study the ruggedly handsome man standing in front of her. She had guessed from the moment she heard his commanding Texas accent on the other side of her door just who had sent him. One look at the leather aviator jacket, Western-cut cotton shirt, worn jeans and boots had told the rest of the story. Her brother, Howard, had tired of her ignoring his phone messages, letters and e-mails, and had sent this good-looking stud to get her. Too bad said stud didn't yet know he was on a fool's errand.

"Let me guess," she murmured, looking him up and down while trying not to be taken in by his broad shoulders, taut abs and six-foot-three frame. The mussed sable hair, smoky blue eyes and intractable jaw were a little harder to disregard. This was a man who was used to getting what he wanted, when he wanted it, and what he intended to retrieve now was her. Not that she planned to cooperate, she reminded herself.

"You're a bodyguard."

"Close."

She studied the short hair and rigid posture. "Cop?"

"Ex-military." Will cast another look at the mouse. Satisfied all was status quo—at least for the moment—he looked back at her. "The law enforcement officer in my family is my brother Kevin, who's a sheriff's deputy."

She really didn't want to know that. Didn't want to get involved with anyone connected with her brother. Still, curious as ever, she had to ask, "What was your MOS in the service?"

"Pilot."

Of course. "Branch?"

"United States Navy."

She sighed. Another link to Howard and the sea and a lot of things she didn't want to think about. She lifted a hand. "I see."

He eyed her skeptically. "You were supposed to know I was coming."

Shrugging, she tightened her hands on the broom. "My brother left a message on my answering machine that he was going to provide transportation to Texas for me."

Will flashed her a sexy smile. "And I'm the pilot of that private jet."

Samantha tore her gaze from the sensual shape of his lower lip and concentrated on the straight line of his nose. "Too bad you wasted a trip."

He didn't seem to think so. "We can talk about that later,"

he assured her, clamping a friendly hand on her shoulder. "Right now I suggest we work on capturing Mickey Mouse before he makes a run for it again."

Ignoring the warmth transmitting to her skin, Samantha studied the strong column of his throat and the soft hair visible in the open collar of his shirt. She stepped back, breaking their connection. "You've got an idea, I suppose?"

Will took his time surveying their surroundings. "That's right. But first we're going to need a deep container—like that trash can—to put him in."

Samantha walked over to the tall plastic container that had been with her since her college days. "It doesn't have a lid."

Will inspected the makeshift detention center. "We don't need a lid if it's empty. Mice can't jump more than a foot or so."

Will McCabe had an air of authority—Samantha gave him that. With effort, she suppressed a shudder at her next supposition. "You're sure he can't just run up the sides?"

Sheer male confidence radiated from the Texan. "No more than you or me."

Samantha wanted to trust Will McCabe. She couldn't. Not when just the idea of that mouse on the loose again had her contemplating a leap into his strong arms. "How do you know?" she challenged, looking deep into his blue eyes.

His lips took on a rueful tilt and he gestured vaguely. "Let's just say I, too, haven't always lived in the best places."

Good to know.

Preferring Will in the line of fire rather than herself, Samantha took out the plastic sack lining the trash can, and tied it shut. Her anxiety building once again, she carried the empty can to him.

Will took off his leather jacket and rolled up the sleeves of his cotton shirt. "You need to step back."

Samantha didn't know whether to laugh or run for cover,

given how wily and agile the mouse had been thus far. "You're going to do this all by yourself, I suppose," she stated dryly.

He shifted his stance. "Yep."

Samantha positioned herself a safe distance away and folded her arms. "This I have to see."

Without missing a beat, Will swiftly moved the sofa from the wall, reached down and grabbed the exposed mouse by the tail, then dropped it into the garbage can. That quickly, the problem was resolved; the mouse that had terrorized her for a week was in rodent jail.

Feeling more than a little foolish for all her antics with the broom, Samantha stared at Will.

"Mind if I wash my hands?" he asked.

"Go right ahead," she murmured, peering into the trash can. The mouse was scampering about in a panic, but every time it tried to get up the sides, it fell back to the bottom. About three inches long, with its tail another four inches, it looked harmless enough.

Her heart still racing, Samantha glanced at Will. She sensed they weren't out of the woods yet. "Now what?" she demanded.

He sauntered to the kitchen sink and turned on the faucet. "You need to take the mouse at least a half mile away if you don't want him visiting you again. And you need to plug up any openings larger than a quarter inch if you want to avoid any more 'company.'"

After glancing again at the little critter, Samantha edged closer to Will. "Plug the holes with what?" She watched him pump a generous amount of antibacterial soap in his palm, then start scrubbing his large, square hands.

"A mixture of steel wool and caulking compound works best," he said with a grin. "Got either here?"

Flushing from the close quarters, Samantha knelt beside him to check beneath the sink. Too late, she remembered how scantily dressed she was. "Actually, both." She wondered if it would be too obvious if she went and put on a robe. Then again, he had already seen her in her nightshirt and hard-soled hiking boots.

He stepped slightly to one side and looked down at her, clearly oblivious to the reason behind her indecision. "Get 'em out," he told her gently. "And I'll do it for you."

Trying not to think about his denim-covered thighs, Samantha stood. There was no reason solid male muscle should be such a turn-on. She swallowed to ease the parched feeling in her throat. "You're awfully nice." She handed over the items he requested.

He lifted a brow, bemused. "And that's a surprise because?" His voice dropped another notch.

Feeling her cheeks heat all the more, she pulled a spackling tool from a drawer. Their fingers collided as she handed it over, his warm hand brushing hers. "You're an associate of my brother's."

Will looked at her but made no comment. Inexplicably, Samantha was flooded with guilt. She pushed it away, prepared to stand her ground. "But just because I appreciate your assistance," she continued frankly, "does not mean I'm going to Laramie with you. Because I'm not."

He gazed at her another long moment.

She could have sworn he was disappointed.

"Suit yourself," he said finally.

Samantha sighed, hating the guilt flowing through her once again. She had no reason to feel beholden to her brother after the way Howard had treated her. And yet… "You think I'm being unreasonable, don't you?" she asked.

Will's broad shoulders lifted and fell. Holding her eyes deliberately, he replied, "Let's just say I know when a lady is doing herself in—repeatedly."

Anger knotted her gut. "You don't know our history."

He scanned the baseboard until he found a place that needed

patching. "Sure I do." He knelt down in front of it and pried open the can of spackle. "You and Howard were both orphaned when you were kids." Will removed the lid, set it aside, then stuck the putty knife in the compound. "He couldn't take care of you and you ended up in foster care. You've never forgiven him."

Samantha sighed. So many people thought that. So many people were wrong. "Howard could have taken care of me," she fumed, as the old bitterness came back to haunt her. Deciding she needed more cover, anyway, she walked into the bathroom and snatched her plaid flannel robe off the hook on the door. Struggling into it, she walked back out. "He was eighteen."

Will cast her a censoring look before he pressed steel wool into the small hole, then covered it with caulking compound. "And you were eight, Samantha."

His calmness in the face of her pain sent her temper soaring. Samantha stomped nearer, her heavy boots slapping against the scarred wood floor. "So? He could have gotten a job!" She pushed the words through clenched teeth. "Found us an apartment or something." *Had Howard wanted to do so*, she amended silently. To her heartbreak, her brother hadn't.

Will sat back on his haunches and looked at her with sympathy. "Howard was little more than a kid himself," he pointed out.

"And that gave him the right to join the navy? To go off for months and months and months at a time?" Her voice choked at the memory. "I cried my eyes out, missing him."

Will rose to his feet, every inch of him lithe and masculine. "And you still are, from the looks of it," he noted softly. Finding another mousehole, he began patching that, too.

Agitated to even be having this conversation, never mind with someone as handsome and commanding as Will McCabe, Samantha paced back and forth. She pressed her lips together mutinously. "I gave up crying over my big brother years ago."

"Then why is the idea of going back to Texas to see him so threatening?" Will challenged.

She clenched her fists, watching as he located and filled yet another gap in the baseboard. "It's not," she declared, telling herself it was her tension causing her heart to pound and her mouth to go dry, and not his nearness.

Will looked at her as if she had either lost her mind or was a disaster waiting to happen. He smirked. "Then prove it."

"I don't have to prove anything to you."

"True." He rose slowly and squared off with her. "But you've got a heck of a lot to prove to yourself."

She lifted her chin. "I do not."

He flashed a goading half smile, then headed back to the kitchen to put the patching compound and steel wool in the cupboard beneath the sink. As he bent over, she was treated to the sight of his denim-covered backside. Then he straightened and pivoted toward her. "You're just afraid that if you give yourself a chance, you're going to end up loving your brother as much as everybody else who knows him."

Samantha wished Will McCabe didn't look so darn sexy, with the faint shadow of an evening beard covering his face. She told him smugly, "Not very likely."

"If you say so."

Their eyes met. A sizzling attraction flowed between them. "Are you about done?" Samantha asked hotly.

"With sealing up the place?" He deliberately misunderstood the question—just to annoy her, she was fairly sure. "Yep, but not," he qualified, his gaze trailing over her hair, face and lips with disturbing thoroughness before returning to her eyes, "with talking sense into you."

SAMANTHA ARCHED A BROW. "You are not going to get me to change my mind."

Determined to have his way on this whether she liked it or

not, Will suggested, "How about we make a deal then? I'll take Mickey Mouse here out of this apartment and set him free in a park on the way to the airport if you come to Texas with me."

"That's not a bargain," she declared with a tight smile, getting another trash bag out from under the sink.

"Could have fooled me," Will quipped.

She opened the bag up and began throwing away cereal boxes with the bottoms eaten out of them. "That's blackmail."

Will had never failed to complete a mission. He wasn't going to do it now, even if she had forgotten how to trust. Seeing a pretzel bag that had been munched on, too, he added it to the trash. "So you admit you're afraid of mice."

She stared at him for a long moment. "I like to keep my distance from anything that skulks around where it has no business being."

Meaning him, Will thought with a smile. He shrugged. "Okay. See ya." He picked up his jacket and headed for the door.

She rushed after him. "Wait." Her fingertips brushed his arm.

He turned, inhaling the faint scent of lavender again.

As he had hoped, practicality overrode pride. "I'm not going to be able to talk a cab driver into letting me into his vehicle with a live mouse in a trash can. It's just not going to happen. Not in New York City. Not tonight."

Will draped his jacket over his shoulder, then stroked the corner of his mouth with his thumb, prepared to make this either as difficult or as easy as she wanted it to be. "Not a problem for me," he told her carelessly. "I've got a limo idling at the curb."

Her lips pursed in a pretty scowl. "I hope Howard is paying for that."

No doubt about it, she wanted retribution. "He is. And," Will added, "he's prepared to do a lot more by way of penance. All you have to do is come to Texas with me and see him."

She shook her head. "Like I said, not an option."

"Then we're at a standstill, aren't we?"

She paused as if to consider her options, then finally laid on the charm. "Are you sure you can't just…take care of this for me?" she asked sweetly, flipping back her lustrous hair.

Figuring she didn't try the femme fatale routine very often, Will remained steadfast. He shook his head. "You know the terms."

Samantha folded her arms and leaned toward him, far from oblivious to the way her stance was lifting the soft curves of her breasts. "And you know I can't agree to those terms, on principle."

"Then you're just flat out of luck, aren't you?"

She released a long-suffering sigh and pursed her lips again. "Look." She moved one hand in a graceful gesture, not about to give up. "You seem like a nice man."

Who was about to be played by one hell of a Texas beauty. "So you said," Will drawled.

The smile she gave him was infinitely seductive. "Can't you just convince my brother that I don't want anything to do with him and let that be that?"

Wishing he could act on instinct, forget his mission and make a move on her, Will shook his head. There would be no hauling her into his arms and kissing her, now or any other time, he warned himself sternly. No blurring of boundaries. No action on his part that would give her an excuse to run the other way from the only family she had left.

"Surely if you told Howard how opposed I am to any reunion, he'd believe you. And let this ridiculous notion of his go."

Will once again shook his head. "That's something you need to tell Howard yourself, face-to-face."

Her lower lip took on a kissable pout. "I can't go to Texas because I don't have the money to come back."

Will had already suspected that she was short of cash. "Howard said something about you being let go from your job last September."

Her cheeks turned pink with humiliation. Looking more miserable than ever, she dropped the temptress act and shoved a hand through her thick, glossy brown hair. "My brother knows I was laid off by the advertising agency?" she probed.

Will edged closer. "Yep, which is part of why Howard wants to see you so badly. He wants to make sure you're all right."

Samantha scowled. "He wants me to settle in Texas."

Will could see her there, too. In jeans, boots, a snap-front Western shirt and a hat that was all attitude. With family nearby. He closed the distance between them, not stopping until they were nose to nose. "Would that be such a bad thing?"

"Yes." The look in her eyes grew turbulent. "All the best advertising jobs are here."

Will leaned toward her ear and whispered conspiratorially, "So don't move back there." Ready to play peacemaker if it would end the decade-long feud between Howard and Samantha, he advised, "Just go see him. Tell him you're no longer family and never will be again, if that's what you want. When you've said your piece, I'll fly you back here from Texas."

Samantha scoffed. "I can guarantee you he won't pay for that."

Will gave a careless shrug. "Doesn't need to—I can fly one of my jets here whenever I want."

"You have more than one?" she asked in an interested tone.

"Six," he confirmed, happy to see that she appeared as impressed as he was by his hard-won success. "And ten pilots," he continued, "although a couple of them only work part-time."

He could see she was on the brink.

"You should do this, Samantha," he urged, using every bit of persuasion in his arsenal. He cupped her shoulders lightly. "Family is important."

She exhaled deeply, unbearable sadness coming into her pretty eyes. Then she stepped away, undeterred. "I just wish I had one."

# Chapter Two

"Second thoughts?" Will asked, emerging from the cockpit several hours later.

Samantha did not know how the sexy pilot had read her mind—she'd spent years perfecting her poker face. To the point that most people hadn't a clue what she was thinking or feeling. Will McCabe not only spotted her vulnerabilities, he seemed determined to get around them. She unclasped her seat belt and stood. "About succumbing to your persuasive ways?"

He opened the hatch that also served as the staircase, then watched as she squared her shoulders and slung her purse over her shoulder.

"It's not going to be that bad," he told her with a wry smile.

Unsure whether it was resentment or nerves twisting her stomach into knots, Samantha countered, "You don't know that."

"Sure I do." He carried her small suitcase down the steps, then waited for her at the bottom.

Together, they walked across the tarmac toward the hangar.

He reached over and gave her elbow a companionable squeeze. "'Cause I know Howard."

Another reason why not to develop any kind of friendship or camaraderie with this man, she thought, since his primary allegiance was clearly to her estranged older brother. Not to her, no matter how chivalrous he was acting. Trying not to think about the way her skin was tingling from just that brief, casual contact, Samantha drew a stabilizing breath. "Let's get this over with," she muttered, spotting the silhouette of a man coming out of the brightly lit building in front of them.

Samantha hadn't seen Howard in close to ten years, but she would have known her brother anywhere. He had the same tall, lithe build, dark hair and eyes that she did.

Howard closed the distance between them quickly. He started to hug her, but read her reserve and changed his mind. He moved back awkwardly, then looked her in the eye with a sincerity and warmth she found disquieting. "I'm glad you could come," he told her, as Will looked on, clearly uncomfortable being put in the middle of this family drama.

Feeling unaccountably glad that Will was with her, so she didn't have to face this alone, Samantha turned her attention back to Howard. She studied the gray at his temples. That and the crow's-feet around his eyes were the only signs that her brother had just turned forty. She forced herself not to see the similarities to both their parents. Or the regret on his face. He'd hurt her badly. She wasn't going to let him do it again. "What's this about?" she asked wearily.

Howard's mouth took on a determined slant. "I think it's time we ended this cold war between us."

That, they could have said on the phone. Had she picked up, which she wouldn't have.

Ignoring the wordless entreaty from Will to cooperate, Samantha shrugged. "Well, I don't."

Will set her suitcase down beside her. "If you need me, I'll be in the office," he said.

Samantha latched on to his arm before he could depart, and reeled him back to her side. "I need you now."

Will lifted a brow at her and gave Howard a glance. Her

brother shrugged. "I don't mind if you hear everything we say, as long as I get to say it."

She added, "And I don't want to be alone with him."

Will gave Howard a look that let his friend know he was doing this against his better judgment, and Samantha one that told her she was being childish. She didn't care. Hardening her heart against further devastation was the only way she had survived the years of abandonment and crushing disappointment.

Annoyed that Will wasn't giving her the emotional backup she needed, Samantha removed her fingers from his taut biceps. She turned back to Howard, enunciating firmly, "The only reason I came was to give you the closure you seem to need, so you'll leave me alone." *Forever.*

Howard held his arms wide. "I don't want closure. I want a new beginning."

Samantha shook her head, her customary stubbornness rising up to give her strength. She pushed the words between clenched teeth. "Not going to happen, bro."

"At least meet my fiancée," Howard insisted, with a combination of firmness and hope.

*Fiancée?* The news that her brother was engaged hit Samantha like a sucker punch to the gut. Though why it should… She stared at him in shock, even as unexpected moisture gathered behind her eyes. "You—the guy who has run from every familial obligation for years—is getting married?" She couldn't believe he was up for such a heavy-duty, lifelong commitment. Didn't want to believe it.

Howard nodded, suddenly looking as emotional as she felt. "To Molly Weatherby," he admitted in a low, choked voice. Blinking rapidly, he cleared his throat. "She's a wonderful woman. I think you'll like her, and she's very anxious to meet you."

Aware that Will was gauging her reaction every bit as carefully as her brother was, Samantha regained her composure with effort. "Clearly, Molly doesn't understand our dynamic," she said sweetly.

Will lifted his brow again. Samantha ignored the powerful censure radiating from him.

As did Howard. "Have dinner with us tomorrow," he pressed.

And open the door to further demands she had no desire to meet? Samantha thought bitterly. She wasn't that much of a fool. It had been a mistake coming here in the first place. She shook her head and stepped back, away from both men. "I'm leaving in the morning, come hell or high water."

"Then we'll make it breakfast," Howard insisted, with the same polite do-or-die attitude that had made him such a success as an investment banker. "Please, Samantha," he continued in a quiet tone that tugged on her heartstrings. "Do this for me."

Samantha supposed this could provide much needed closure for both of them. "Fine. Whatever." Her voice was as cool as she could make it. "Just so you know this is the last time you and I are going to be seeing each other." She regarded her brother steadily. "There'll be no more messages on my machine, no more letters, no more hunky pilots kicking down my front door to save me."

Now Howard looked at Will with silent reproach.

He held up a hand like a traffic cop. "Long story," he muttered.

To her surprise, Howard simply nodded.

Pulse pounding, Samantha looked around, desperate for escape. "Is there a ladies' room handy?"

Will pointed toward a corner of the brightly lit hangar. " To the left there's a unisex."

"Thanks." Head down against the warm Texas wind, Samantha hurried off.

She barely made it through the door of the concrete-floored building before bursting into tears she didn't want and couldn't explain.

"I'M STILL AMAZED YOU GOT her here," Howard told Will as the two of them walked across the tarmac, following the path Samantha had taken.

So was he, if truth be told. Will thought about the sentimental tears Samantha had blinked back. He had learned a long time ago to pay more attention to what people did than what they said. It was actions, not speeches, that told the tale. He looked at the bathroom door, which was still closed, and led the way to his glass-walled office. "I don't think there is any doubt that Samantha wants to reconcile with you," he told his old friend kindly.

The confidence Howard had displayed in the presence of his sister faded. In its place were soul-deep regret and frustration. "Be honest, man. She hates my guts."

"Yeah." Will sank down in the battered chair behind his equally beat-up metal desk. "But she loves you, too, otherwise she wouldn't have come this far." She would have grabbed her mouse and told Will to take a flying leap back to Texas, instead of allowing him to coax her into coming.

Too wound up to sit, Howard paced across the small, square space. He paused in front of the window overlooking the runway. "My sister's right about one thing." He shoved his hands through his hair, then clasped the back of his neck. "I let her down."

A veteran of all sorts of domestic difficulties, Will propped his boots on the edge of his desk. "It happens, even in the best families. It doesn't mean you can't make it up to her."

Howard turned away from the view of the dark Texas sky, his expression bleak. "In the course of one reluctantly-consented-to breakfast?" he asked skeptically.

Will gestured for him to take a seat in one of the military-surplus chairs. "She'll end up staying however long it takes."

Howard sank down with a sigh. "She'll never agree to that."

*Oh ye of little faith.* "I'll soften her up and keep her entertained while she's in Laramie," Will promised.

His friend perked up a bit. "You'd do that for me?"

"Even more." Will grinned. "I owe you for helping me get my business off the ground."

Feminine footsteps sounded on the concrete floor. Seconds later, Samantha strode in. She looked composed again, but her eyes were rimmed with red, as if she'd been crying. Will felt for her. He knew this had to be hard. He also knew it had to be done.

"It's late," she said, before either man could speak. "And I'm exhausted. If one of you could point me toward the closest hotel…"

Will and Howard exchanged uneasy looks.

"What?" she demanded.

Howard risked her wrath and informed her reluctantly, "The state agricultural extension service is holding their spring workshops here in Laramie for the next two weeks. People come from all over West Texas to attend them. All the hotel rooms for miles around are booked. But not to worry," he assured her. "I've got the guest room made up."

She should have been trapped, albeit nicely, into spending more time with the only family she had. Will had to hand it to Samantha; she didn't miss a beat. "Thanks," she said with a breezy smile, "but I'm staying the night with Will."

He looked at her, making no effort to hide his surprise.

Howard frowned. "You can't do that," he argued.

She tilted her head to one side. "Want to bet?"

Doing his best to help his friend, Will murmured, "Your brother is right, Samantha. His place is so much nicer. You'll be a lot more comfortable there."

She dug in her heels. "I don't require fancy digs. Your place is fine."

Will decided to let her have her way—temporarily. It

wouldn't take her long to cry uncle, once she realized what she had done. "My place it is, then."

The glint in Howard's eyes said he had an idea what Will was up to.

Playing along, Howard turned back to his sister with a poker face. "I'll see you in the morning at my house then," he stated, cordial as ever.

Distracted, Samantha nodded her assent.

Once again, Howard started to hug his little sister, then decided against it and just walked out.

Will and Samantha were left facing each other.

"Let's go, then," she said. She slung the small carry-on bag over her arm. "Like I said, I'm exhausted."

Curious as to what her reaction was going to be, Will gestured toward the metal stairs just outside his office door. "After you."

Samantha blinked in confusion. "What are you talking about?"

He pointed to the closed door above them. "That's where I live."

SAMANTHA WOULD HAVE thought Will McCabe was joking, had it not been for the way too innocent, I'm-just-giving-you-what-you-asked-for expression on his face.

*I can handle this. It's just for one night. Then I'll have met any last-ditch familial obligation. I can go back to New York City and get on with my life.* Determined not to let Will McCabe's shenanigans get to her, Samantha turned and headed up the stairs. He followed lazily behind, and his shoulder brushed hers when he unlocked the door and swung it open.

Samantha stared at the sparse decor.

"Not too late to change your mind," Will told her. "I bet Howard is only a mile or so down the road by now. You can call him on his cell, ask him to double back and get you."

Which was clearly what the two men had planned all along, Samantha thought. No wonder they had sent each other those indecipherable looks! They had to have known how shocked and dismayed she would be.

"This is fine," she fibbed. So what if it was one large room with a cement floor and walls? Technically, it had everything she needed. A hot plate, small fridge, microwave. Television with satellite receiver. Stereo. Adjoining bath, with shower stall. She pivoted back to Will and tossed him a devil-may-care smile. "Just one question. Where are *you* going to sleep?"

Will locked eyes with her. He hooked his thumbs through the belt loops on either side of his fly. "Here."

*Right.*

"I hate to break it to you," Samantha replied dryly, "but that's a metal army cot."

He turned to look, as if he had never seen it before. "Uh-huh."

Aware that he was being deliberately dense just to get under her skin, she elaborated, "For one."

A sexy grin spread across his face. "Then I guess we'll be real cozy, huh?"

Samantha gave him a look that let him know they would not be hooking up, tonight or at any other time. "Surely you can sleep on the plane," she said.

His expression gave away nothing. "Surely you can sleep at your brother's place."

Beginning to lose patience despite herself, Samantha jabbed a thumb at her chest. "Then *I'll* sleep on the jet."

He vetoed her idea. "It's either here—in that bed—with me," he told her flatly, "or at Howard's."

It seemed Samantha had been searching her whole life for a man every bit as stubborn and strong-willed as she was. Finally, she'd found one. The only trouble was they had very different ideas about what should happen next.

She edged closer. "Even a car or pickup would do." She'd learned to get comfortable anywhere and appreciate the roof over her head.

"You're not sleeping in a vehicle, either."

Samantha's heartbeat quickened. "Says who?"

"Me," he replied with exaggerated seriousness.

"You can't tell me what to do," Samantha declared, ignoring the tingling sensation that started up inside her whenever he was near.

"I don't have to provide you with the keys to my pickup truck, either." He regarded her smugly. "So it looks like you're back to plan A. Bunking with your brother."

Samantha flushed. "Absolutely not!"

He looked at his watch. "Five seconds to change your mind."

She glowered at him.

With a shrug, Will said, "All right, then." He strolled over to the row of metal clothes lockers against the wall. Opening one, he pulled out boxers and a T-shirt fresh from the laundry. "I'm going to bed."

Samantha's jaw dropped. She knew Will was a no-rules kind of guy, but this was beyond ridiculous! "You can't be serious."

"Afraid I am." He gave her a thorough once-over that had her insides fluttering.

Refusing to let him get to her, she merely lifted a brow in return.

The tension between them ratcheted up another notch.

She knew he was thinking about the sexual implications of the hours ahead, as was she.

"You're not getting lucky."

"I figured," he replied.

"So maybe you'd better bunk elsewhere."

"Don't think so. I like my quarters and my bed just fine."

Another stalemate.

She was definitely losing this battle.

Will made a great show of yawning. "If you want to brush your teeth or change into something more comfortable, better do it. Then it's going to be lights out."

Samantha knew he still expected her to give in and run to her brother. No way that was happening. He thought he could be difficult? So could she.

"First dibs on the bathroom," she countered.

With amusement tugging at his lips, he lounged against the wall. "Have at it."

All too aware of his gaze tracking her every step, Samantha rolled her carry-on suitcase into the bathroom. Ignoring the slight trembling of her fingers, she locked the door behind her and changed into the lavender sleep shirt she had been wearing when Will had kicked in her door. Then she washed her face and brushed her teeth in record time.

Truth to tell, she *was* exhausted. She didn't care where she slept as long as she had a place to rest her head. And she was still hoping Will McCabe's gentlemanly instincts would kick in—surely the aggravating man had some!—and he would go elsewhere to sleep.

Finished, she crammed everything back in her suitcase, sauntered out and looked at Will—then felt her mouth go dry.

He had stripped down to his jeans. Raw power radiated from his tall, extraordinarily fit frame.

So much for the hope he'd make a chivalrous exit, Samantha thought.

He really intended to spend the night with her on that tiny bed! Unless...he was calling her bluff?

Pretending she wasn't turned on at the sight of all that hard muscle and abundant masculinity, Samantha inclined her head in the direction of the bath. "It's all yours."

He ambled past, T-shirt and shorts still clutched in one hand. The door shut and the shower went on.

Not sure whether to be grateful for the respite or worried about what would happen if he really decided to sleep in the single bed next to her, Samantha sighed and climbed beneath the covers—a starched white sheet and green wool blanket. She put her head down, just for a second, and closed her eyes.

The next thing she knew the bathroom door opened and a wedge of light spilled into the room. Will strode out, clad in his boxers and T-shirt, then switched off the light. She caught a whiff of man and soap as he slid in beside her, rolled onto his back and locked his hands behind his head. Wedged between the wall and his body, Samantha had nowhere to go. Worse, she was lying on her side, facing him. A position that was far too…intimate.

She turned, bumping her knee against his rock-hard thigh and her elbow against his chest. Her sleep shirt rode up. She tugged it down, then tried easing onto her back so she, too, would be staring up at the ceiling. His shoulders were so wide the two of them didn't quite fit. She took a deep breath. "Could you turn on your side?"

"Sure." He rolled to face her.

Heavens, he was a handful. "I meant the other way."

His broad chest rumbled with suppressed laughter. "I know what you meant."

Samantha set her jaw. And tried not to think about kissing him. Passionately, and without restraint. "You're not going to cooperate with me, are you?" she asked irritably.

He gave her an innocent look. "This is me, cooperating."

And she thought she'd known trouble before. "Forget it." Samantha bumped bodies with him again, shifting around until she was on her side, facing the wall. They had maybe an inch between them. She could still fell the heat emanating from his skin. Hear his deep, even breathing.

Knowing this had been a gigantic mistake on her part, but not about to admit it, she closed her eyes and tried to relax. Unsuccessfully. Yet before long she could tell, from the sound of Will's breathing, that he was asleep.

She was safe. There'd be no more verbal sparring, no more quietly searching looks, no more attempts to figure her out, for at least a few hours. Just blissful rest with a strong, capable man lying beside her.

She ought to feel relieved at the respite from all the emotional stuff.

So why didn't she?

Will awoke at shortly after six in the morning. Remaining perfectly still, he looked at the woman beside him. She was sleeping soundly, her body not touching his. It hadn't been that way all night, he recalled, with a strange mix of feelings. At around 2:00 a.m. he had wakened to the sound of a soft gasp and a slight vibration of the bed. It had taken him a minute to realize the shaking was in her chest. Samantha hadn't struck him as a woman who did a lot of crying—if any—so the sight of the hand pressed to her mouth and the tears running down her face, as she struggled to suppress any signs of weakness, even in sleep, had made his own gut tighten.

Howard had told Will that his kid sister had had one hell of a childhood after their parents died, and it was all Howard's fault.

Will knew what it was like to lose a parent. Samantha had lost both, plus her only brother, all at once. She'd survived by becoming tough. But that toughness was cracking under the stress of all that had happened to her recently….

Samantha stirred and turned, elbowing him sharply in the chest. Will grunted, and the noise woke her. She looked startled, as if she didn't know where she was or how the hell he happened to be there. Sure he couldn't handle an assault on his ears before he'd had coffee, he cupped a hand lightly over her mouth, in case she screamed. "It's okay."

A pleat formed between her brows as reality slowed dawned. "Says you. I'm stiff all over." She moaned. "I need to get up."

So did he. All this shifting around had made him think of things he didn't need to be thinking about. He threw back the covers, eased off the mattress, stood and offered her a hand up.

Too late, he noticed that her sleep shirt had twisted around her waist, revealing black French-cut panties and a perfect body. Flushing, she scrambled to cover herself, while he got a clean pair of jeans from the row of metal lockers that served as his closet, and pretended he hadn't seen. "I've got to go talk to my mechanic." Will grabbed a shirt and boots and headed out the door.

An hour later, he had finished touching base with everyone who worked for him when Samantha walked into his office, looking gorgeous in a sophisticated black turtleneck sweater and slacks that would have been right for a New York spring day, but were way too hot for April in Texas. "How do I get to this breakfast with my brother?"

Happy to see her looking like herself again, he rose. "I'll escort you."

She peered at him skeptically. "You will?"

He reached for his keys. "Sure. Got to eat. Molly's a heck of a cook."

"Fine," she muttered, running a hand through her wavy brown hair. "Then we head back to New York?"

"I told you I'd take you," Will confirmed.

*I just didn't say exactly when.*

# Chapter Three

"You ever been to Laramie before?" Will asked from behind the wheel of his extended-cab pickup truck.

Samantha turned her gaze to peaceful tree-lined streets, a beautiful downtown district with historic buildings and a mixture of quaint and modern businesses. This was the West Texas of travel brochures, complete with a movie production studio helmed by legendary actor-director Beau Chamberlain, and a garment factory that produced Jenna Lockhart clothing. They passed the Lone Star Dance Hall, the limestone county courthouse and the community hospital before turning onto Houston Street. Restored Victorian houses sat on elegantly manicured lawns. Spring was in full bloom, as attested by the colorful flower beds and leafy trees.

Aware that Will was waiting for an answer, Samantha replied, "No. I've never been in this part of the state." Emerging from the vehicle, she spoke above the sounds of a lawn mower one block over. "I grew up in Beaumont. Left Texas the year I turned eighteen. Never to return, until now." Now that she was back, soaking up the distinctive Lone Star ambience, she wondered if that might not have been a mistake. There was something about this part of the country that felt familiar and much more comforting than she could have imagined.

Will met up with her at the bumper. He slid a hand beneath

her elbow as they moved up the walk toward the pine-green frame home with white shutters and trim. "You went to NYU on scholarship, right?"

Trying not to think how much this reminded her of the home she'd grown up in, albeit on a much grander scale, Samantha eased away from his touch. "How'd you know that?"

Will shoved his hands in his pockets. "Howard told me. He thought it was because you wanted to be near him, since he was working for an investment banking firm on Wall Street back then."

If anything, that had been a major deterrent, Samantha recalled with the bitter resentment that had haunted her for years. "Not quite," she clarified. "That just happened to be where I got the best scholarship."

The front door opened. A petite woman with short, curly red hair and flushed cheeks emerged. She had a smudge of flour on her chin and a welcoming light in her eyes. In contrast to Samantha's brother, who was dressed like the investment banker he was, Molly wore jeans, a turquoise Western shirt and boots. Samantha had been prepared not to like her any more than she liked her brother. That was impossible, she soon found.

"Howdy, y'all!" Molly beamed, enveloping her in the kind of fierce, familial hug Samantha hadn't had since she was eight. "Welcome!"

Molly ushered them in, leading the way through the spacious country kitchen at the rear of the home, to the slate-floored, screened-in porch overlooking the backyard. "I'm so glad you agreed to be in our wedding!"

Shocked by the assumption, Samantha took a step back and bumped into Will's chest. His hand came up to steady her.

Howard sent an apologetic look at his bride-to-be. "I haven't asked her yet."

An uncomfortable silence fell over the group. Molly looked

back at Samantha with an expression of longing for acceptance that Samantha understood only too well.

"Then *I* will," Molly told him softly, clearly not understanding why Howard had delayed on this. "Samantha, we both would like it very much if you would be my maid of honor. It would be wonderful to have you as part of our wedding party. You've already met Will here—he's the best man."

Yet another reason why she should decline the invitation, Samantha thought.

The four of them sat down at a beautifully set wicker-and-glass table. "That's very sweet of you to ask," she hedged as they passed the dishes around, family style.

"It would mean so much to us," Molly stated, the yearning for family plain in her eyes. "To me, especially, since you'll be my first—my only—sister."

Samantha had always wanted a sister, too. But becoming close to Molly meant being near her brother, as well.

Determined not to bring Molly into their feud, she gestured apologetically. "It's not really a good time." She tried not to think how long it had been since she'd had sausage and biscuits with homemade cream gravy. She knew she'd never had any quite this delicious, and the same went for the fruit compote and freshly brewed coffee. "I'm looking for a job right now."

Compassion radiated from Molly's eyes. "Howard told me you'd been laid off."

Samantha swore silently to herself. She hadn't wanted her brother to know. Doing her best to disguise her wounded pride, she turned to Howard.

He shrugged. "When you didn't return my calls, I telephoned you at Gallimore, Smith & Tomberlin, and found you hadn't been employed there for six months."

A flush of embarrassment heated Samantha's cheeks. *Great. One more humiliation, added to the heap.*

She regarded the others at the table with a great deal more

confidence than she felt. "I've been looking." She'd gone door to door to every ad agency in the city, and even ventured into Jersey, passing out résumés and meeting with human resource directors. "I'm sure I'll find something soon," she stated, knowing darn well that the odds were stacked against her finding a position anywhere near as prestigious as the one she'd had prior to getting involved with Shawn.

"You could look in Texas," Molly suggested. "Or start your own advertising agency in Laramie County. I mean, I know it's not the New York City ad world, but there's plenty of work locally to be had by an enterprising individual. There isn't an advertising agency for a hundred miles, so people either have to travel several hours to meet with someone, or do it themselves. Neither option is ideal."

"I'm sure you're right, but with several irons in the fire, I have to go back to New York."

Molly understood, even as she refused to take no for an answer. "The wedding is this weekend. You can stay until then, can't you?" She clasped Samantha's hand. "It's only seven days, and it would mean so much to us. Howard even has a car for you to drive if you stay," Molly added. "That white Lexus coupe parked next to the house."

Will squinted at the vehicle, just visible from where they were seated. "It looks brand-new," he remarked.

"It is." Molly got up to pour more coffee for everyone. "Howard just picked it up in San Angelo a few weeks ago."

Will glanced in Samantha's direction. She knew what he was thinking. It was a question city folk often got. "Yes, I know how to drive," she informed him. "I learned when I was in Texas. I took driver's ed in school—a pilot program paid for my car insurance." Otherwise, as a foster kid, she wouldn't have been able to afford the liability and accident insurance needed to take driver's training.

"Do you own a car now?" Molly asked, returning to her seat.

"No." Samantha stirred sugar and cream into her coffee. She looked up and found Will's eyes on her once again. "It'd be impractical. I rent one when I need one. Otherwise, I walk or take mass transit."

Molly rested her chin on her hands. "It must be so exciting, living in New York."

*More like lonely*, Samantha thought, since all she did was work. And now, look for a job and chase mice in her tiny apartment.

"Hey now." Will sat back in his chair and stretched his long legs out in front of him, his knee nudging hers under the table in the process. "Don't count Texas out." He winked. "Laramie has its thrills."

Samantha knew one. Will McCabe. Not that she intended to become emotionally involved with him.

"I know this is a lot to lay on you all at once," Howard interjected quietly, "but I promise, if you'll be part of our wedding, I won't bug you to visit us again."

Samantha studied him, for a moment seeing the loving older brother he had once been, instead of the emotionally distant man he'd become, after their parents' death. "You swear?"

He nodded, his eyes holding hers. "I know this is my last chance," he admitted with a sincerity that touched her heart. "I know I have a lot to make up to you. I know there is no reason on this earth you should let me try. But I'd still like that opportunity, Samantha. I'd still like to be the family we should have been to each other all along."

"I WISH WE DIDN'T HAVE TO cut this short," Molly said, an hour later. "But I've got to get over to my office. And Howard has to go into Dallas on business."

"Molly's the mayor of Laramie," Howard explained, wrapping an arm around his fiancée's waist.

She hugged him back and acknowledged with pride, "My

biggest accomplishment thus far has been to convince new businesses—like Howard's and Will's—to base their operations here."

"Howard has his own investment banking business now," Will told Samantha.

How odd, she thought, that everyone knew more about her only remaining kin than she did.

"Before I forget!" Molly snatched a turquoise folder from the console in the foyer. "Here is your schedule of wedding events. The first thing is a fitting at Jenna Lockhart's boutique. It's on Main Street, between West Avenue and Bowie Lane. She'd like you to come over this morning, if you can. Meanwhile…" Molly paused. "Where are you going to stay this week?"

Samantha sensed yet another invitation coming. There was a limit to how much she was going to put herself out there. "With Will," Samantha replied.

"But…" Molly and Howard exchanged concerned looks.

"You'd be more comfortable here," Will pointed out, practical as ever.

Samantha knew that.

"I have a very nice guest room and private bath," Molly added.

Howard held up both hands in a defensive gesture. "Don't worry about running into me. I'm bunking elsewhere until after the wedding," he said.

Knowing the more she accepted from Howard and Molly, the more indebted she would be, Samantha rejected the invitation with a pleasant shake of her head. "Really. Will and I are fine."

"At the airstrip?" Molly appeared unconvinced, as did Howard.

Obviously, Samantha thought ruefully, the two of them had seen Will's Spartan accommodations.

Trying not to think about what it had been like to fall asleep next to Will and wake up in the middle of the night snuggled cozily against him—only to come to her senses and pull away from him once again—Samantha stiffened her spine.

"The accommodations at the airstrip provide absolutely everything I need." Including an incredibly sexy and interesting man to spar with. "So you don't have to worry about me," she said, knowing that much was true, because there was no way she and Will were sharing a bed again. Being so close to each other, even if not so scantily clad, was a temptation neither she nor Will needed.

She might be leading a very celibate existence these days, but she was still human enough to miss the emotional and physical connection that came with making love. Being back in Texas, dealing with her brother, was leaving her vulnerable and overly emotional. Samantha sensed it wouldn't take much more than a few really passionate kisses or a well-timed hug from Will to have her seeing him in a whole new light. And while she guessed hooking up with him would certainly be pleasurable, it wouldn't be smart. When she made love with a man again, she wanted to be in love with him, and most important of all, she wanted him to love her back with all his heart.

"Listen, see y'all later. Thanks for breakfast." Samantha hurried out the door, Will ambling along behind her. He didn't say anything, but she could tell he thought she was behaving foolishly in rejecting Howard and Molly's invitation to stay. For some reason, Will's disapproval bothered her. And that was strange, since she had stopped caring what other people thought about her a long time ago.

Samantha reached the white Lexus being loaned to her. She unlocked the door and was immediately assaulted with the new-car smell.

Aware of Will lingering next to her, Samantha tossed her wedding folder and handbag onto the leather seat. Feeling his eyes upon her, she turned back to him. He came closer still, looking her over from head to toe in a way that electrified her senses. He flashed her a smile.

"How did I just agree to any of this?" she muttered, rolling her eyes. She had promised herself she was returning to Texas only long enough to provide closure and move on. Instead, she had let herself be goaded into spending the night—and sharing a bed!—with a man who was temptation personified, had agreed to meet her brother's fiancée and participate in their wedding, all in a little over thirteen hours. At this rate, who knew what might transpire before the end of the week? If Will McCabe had anything to do with it, quite a lot!

Still studying her, Will put a hand on the top of the coupe. Understanding glimmered in his blue eyes. "Don't beat yourself up about it," he soothed. "Staying is the right thing to do."

Maybe being part of the wedding, giving Howard one last chance to make amends, *was* the right thing to do, Samantha conceded reluctantly. However, continuing to bunk with Will McCabe…well, that was something else entirely. That was courting trouble. He seemed to know it, too.

With effort, Samantha directed her thoughts away from his tantalizing presence and back to the conversation at hand. Just because he had the broadest shoulders and buffest chest she had ever seen—not to mention an Olympic quality lower half—did not mean she had to succumb to temptation.

"The right thing for whom?" she demanded.

"All of you," Will told her. "Like I mentioned earlier, family's important."

Samantha knew that; it was Howard who hadn't. Until now, anyway. It ticked her off that her brother had turned the tables on her, and was now insisting on having what she had so desperately wanted—and given up on ever having.

She crossed her arms and leaned against the open car door. Her heart was beating too fast again, and it was Will's fault. "I don't trust that Howard's not going to hurt me again as soon as this wedding of his is over."

Will rested his hands on her shoulders. "I know him, and I have to tell you that is very unlikely. But even if he tried, Molly would never allow it."

Samantha couldn't disagree with that—Molly was genuine to the core.

Silence fell.

Samantha regarded Will cynically. As much as she would like to let him become her confidant, her protective instincts were warning her against it. Will had made no effort to hide his allegiance to her brother. As kind as he was being to her right now, he was every bit as intent on changing her attitude as Howard was. And for so many reasons, that couldn't happen.

Her momentary desire to cooperate faded as fast as it had appeared. She forced herself to harden her heart. "You knew my brother was getting married this week when you came to get me yesterday."

Will dropped his hands. "It's not exactly a secret."

"You knew he wanted me down here to participate in the ceremony," she accused, feeling more deceived than ever.

She'd gotten used to tending only to her own needs. Will—and Howard and Molly—were trying to bring her out of her shell. She didn't want to complicate her life that way, didn't want to risk being hurt, deserted or betrayed.

He rubbed his jaw contemplatively. "So…?"

Heat rose into her face. "So why didn't you tell me that at the outset?" Samantha demanded, even more upset.

"You wouldn't have come if you'd known he and Molly were going to put you on the spot like that," he stated simply.

"You're darn right I wouldn't have." Samantha dragged the toe of her Italian leather shoe across the paved driveway, no more eager to leave the premises, and end their postbreakfast tête-à-tête, than he apparently was.

"Then it's a good thing I didn't forewarn you." He gave her a wink. "Isn't it?"

Samantha ignored his attempt to tease her back into good humor. "I don't know what I'm going to do," she groused, feeling all the more hot and uncomfortable in clothing that had been designed for an East Coast spring. "I don't have clothes for a week of festivities."

Will checked out her breasts, waist, hips and legs, as if trying to assess her measurements. Imagining what it would be like if he was actually touching instead of just looking, Samantha felt warmth radiate through her. Was it hot out here in the morning sun, or what?

He stepped close enough so she could feel his body heat and breathe in the brisk, masculine fragrance of his cologne. "You could borrow some," he suggested in a low voice. "I've got some sisters-in-law that are about your size. I'm sure they'd be glad to lend you anything you need."

Samantha stiffened. If everyone in Laramie, Texas, was this hospitable, it was going to be hard as heck to leave. Determined not to let him see how much his nearness was affecting her, she lifted a brow.

"I'd rather not be indebted to anyone else here," she said stiffly. Especially since she'd have no way of returning the favor.

Will rocked back on his heels and sent her a flirtatious look that upended her equilibrium even further. "Well, then, buying is an option, too," he drawled. "My brother Lewis's wife, Lexie Remington, designs clothes for young women. Her clothing line is in department stores all over the country now, but she has lots of samples at her design studio that she sells cheaply to locals. All you have to do is make an appointment to go in and see what she has."

Aware that Will was systematically chipping away at her resistance, Samantha wrinkled her nose at him. "That's not the point."

Although the chance to shop at up-and-coming Lexie Reminton's design studio was not to be missed. Samantha already owned a few of her pieces—she'd bought them at Bloomingdale's in Manhattan.

"Then what *is* the point?" he asked.

Not sure when she had felt so off-kilter and aroused all at once, Samantha finally confessed. "I'll go stir-crazy, hanging out here until the wedding." She was used to the hustle and bustle of the city, the anonymity.

"Hey." Will assumed the boldly aggressive stance of a determined salesperson. "You've got plenty to do, besides fulfilling your duties as maid of honor."

"Like what?" she asked.

He moved forward slightly, further invading her space. "For starters, figuring out how you're going to pay me back for your room and board."

She snorted in disbelief. Maybe if she kept the banter up, she wouldn't think about what it was going to be like being in close proximity to Will McCabe for an entire week. "You'd really charge me for sharing a bunk with you?"

He flashed her a grin. "Not monetarily."

Whoa! The images those two words conjured up had her tingling all over. She pushed past him, then remembered she was supposed to be driving away. Getting a grip, she whirled back and decided to take him on, anyway. "I hope you're not suggesting…"

He settled his large frame in the open car door. The look he gave her was direct, uncompromising, confident. Just seeing him that way made her mouth go dry. "My, my, you've got a naughty mind."

Now would have been the perfect time to slip behind the wheel and peel off. Unfortunately, he was blocking her entrance to the driver's side. Furious, she sputtered, "There is no way—"

"Relax." He held up a hand before she could finish her tirade. "I like my women enthusiastic, to say the least."

Samantha imagined they all were, given his ruggedly handsome appearance and easygoing, upbeat attitude.

Feigning disinterest, she rolled her eyes. "Glad we have *that* clear."

He tucked his hands beneath his armpits, and continued watching her in a leisurely fashion that made her think about naked bodies and mussed sheets. "The question remains," he murmured, "how you're going to pay me back for the room and board. In a nonmonetary way, of course."

Samantha sighed, wishing she had never gotten entangled with him.

"Obviously," she retorted, "you have an idea."

"Actually," he replied, "I do. You're an advertising whiz. I have a charter jet service in need of a new ad campaign." He paused to let those two facts sink in. "Think you could put something together for me in a week, between wedding activities?"

Samantha tamped down the immediate spark of excitement she felt. "You're serious." She pretended she wasn't dying for some work.

"Damn right I am," he said with an enticing smile.

She dragged her eyes away from the tempting corners of his mouth, affected her best bored tone. "I guess I could do that for you," she responded, with the same lazy insouciance he was now displaying. "On one condition." She looked deep into his McCabe-blue eyes and paused to let her words sink in. "I want my own bed to sleep in tonight." When that demand looked as if it might be met, she added crisply, "And some sort of comfortable chair to sit in. Plus I'll need access to a desk, your computer and office supplies."

Will responded with a nod and another enigmatic smile. "I'll take care of it right away."

FOUR HOURS LATER, Will had finished making up the flight schedule for the rest of the week and e-mailed it to all his pilots.

He kicked back in his desk chair and folded his hands behind his head.

Samantha strolled in, sunglasses on top of her head. To his surprise, she seemed to get more beautiful every time he laid eyes on her. Why that was so, he couldn't figure out. She was wearing the same sophisticated black clothing that marked her as a city slicker and covered up way too much of her lovely curves. And it wasn't as if she had done anything different to her hair. The thick glossy waves fell unencumbered to her shoulders. She had the same deft touch with makeup. Not that she seemed to use much, from what he had seen. Her eyes were exceptionally captivating in an already gorgeous face—maybe because they seemed wiser than her years. And those lips, Will noted with no small amount of desire, were so soft and luscious looking he was surprised he hadn't figured out a way to kiss them yet.

Not that he couldn't have put the moves on her, had he been so inclined.

He just hadn't wanted to scare her away. Hadn't wanted to risk staking a claim Samantha wasn't ready for. But when she was, he decided, he was definitely going to give it his all. And hope she gave it everything she had, too.

In the meantime, he noticed that she had definitely taken his advice and treated herself. She carried several shopping bags bearing the logos of local boutiques.

Obviously unaware of how his libido amplified at just the sight of her, she dumped the bags in a corner of the room and dropped down in the chair in front of him. The pressure at the front of his jeans increased as she pulled a leather-bound notepad from the oversize leather carryall that passed as her purse.

"Let's get down to business. Show me what you've got."

Irked by her deliberate lack of pleasantries, Will gave her a leisurely once-over meant to get under her skin. Taking his bad behavior a step further, he touched his belt buckle and waggled his brows. "Good thing I know you don't mean that the way it sounds," he drawled.

Behaving as if he hadn't spoken, she offered a tight, officious smile. "If you want me to design an ad campaign," she told him, "I need to review the advertisements you've been running to date."

Impressed by her composure in the wake of his goading, Will opened his center desk drawer and pulled out a thin file folder. He pushed it across his desk. "Here it is."

She snapped it up, then tapped the end of her pen against her lower lip. "I also need current data on your business. Number of planes, pilots, safety record, locations where you fly."

He struggled to keep his mind on business. He should not be thinking about kissing her. "It's all in there, too," he said. "Look on the last page."

For the next few minutes she perused the file, a thoughtful expression on her face. "You are efficient," she said at last.

Maybe it was ego, but he wanted her to appreciate his accomplishments. "Surprised?" he taunted.

She closed the file with a sigh and looked at him. "Only by the pedestrian nature of this newspaper ad you've been running for your company to date. Who designed it, if you don't mind my asking?"

It was hard to be so cocky now. "Me."

She winced slightly, then sat back and recrossed her legs at the knee.

"You don't like it," Will stated, disappointed yet aware she had a point. The latest advertisement hadn't proved very effective in drumming up new business.

Samantha made a seesawing motion with her hand. "Let's just say I think it could be a little more inspired. Not to worry. We'll get there."

Will was sure they would, if Samantha was in the driver's seat. "I like the sound of that." Liked even better the notion that before the day was over he was going to find a way to get her in his arms and kiss her, at least once.

As if noticing the way he was staring at her, Samantha frowned. Before she could ask about it, however, footsteps sounded on the concrete floor outside Will's office.

Oscar Gentry, one of Will's favorite high school teachers, walked in. At age sixty-five, the silver-haired retiree with the kind eyes remained physically fit and well-groomed. But there was an air of desolation about him that Will had never seen before.

Concerned at what could have happened since the last time they'd talked, and hoping he could help the older man the way he'd once helped him, Will pushed himself to his feet and Will came around the desk. "Hi, Mr. Gentry."

"Hello, Will." The man's handshake lacked its usual vigor.

Will touched Samantha's shoulder. "This is Samantha Holmes, Howard's sister."

The distressed look never completely leaving his eyes, Mr. Gentry took Samantha's hand, too. "Here for the wedding?" he asked politely.

She nodded.

"She's also going to devise a new ad campaign for my company," Will added.

Mr. Gentry frowned. "I guess I should have called first. I didn't mean to interrupt."

"It's okay." Will gestured for them all to sit down, then settled behind his desk. "What's up?"

Mr. Gentry adjusted his glasses on his nose. "I took your advice, Will. It didn't work."

Samantha started to rise, sensing that this was a personal matter. "Perhaps I should go."

"Actually—" Mr. Gentry waved his hand, indicating she

should stay right where she was "—I could use a woman's perspective." He pressed his lips together ruefully. "Not that what's going on in my life right now is a big secret, anyway."

Figuring it would be easier for him to explain, Will stated, "Mr. Gentry's wife kicked him out."

The older man ran his hands over his knees. "Yvonne changed the locks on me and everything."

Samantha blinked. "Why?" she asked.

"It's the darnedest thing." He heaved a sigh. "I don't know. I went fishing, just like I do every Saturday morning, and came home to find all the locks were changed, my suitcases packed and on the front porch."

"Had you been fishing a lot?" she asked.

Mr. Gentry shook his head. "No more than usual. Once a week."

"And she never minded before?"

He sighed again. "She said she liked having the time to herself."

Will tapped his pen on the arm of his chair. He looked at Samantha, noting her compassionate expression. "Mr. and Mrs. Gentry's fortieth wedding anniversary is next Sunday. They had a big party planned. Mr. Gentry wants to make up with his wife before then."

The man nodded. "Will told me to get her an apology card from the stationery store and take it to her."

"Along with flowers and candy and her favorite perfume," Will added. When Samantha frowned at him, as if that had been the wrong thing to do, he said defensively, "I figured he should cover all the bases."

"Only it didn't work," Mr. Gentry continued, looking even more miserable. "Yvonne got mad when she read the card, and refused to accept any of my gifts."

Behavior that made no sense at all, Will thought.

Samantha, however, seemed to think it was more a puzzle

to be figured out than an unreasonable response. "And you have no idea why she behaved that way?"

"Yvonne said she needed a specific apology," the former physics teacher revealed in an exasperated tone. "And I told her I can't give her one because I don't know what I've done to tick her off. And then she said that if I didn't know what I'd done, she wasn't going to tell me!'"

Will put his pen down. "I feel for you, pardner."

"The question is—" Mr. Gentry took off his silver-rimmed glasses and rubbed the bridge of his nose in dismay "—what next?"

"You've got to convince her you still love her," Will replied.

"How, when she won't even let me in the door?" he muttered.

Both men turned their gazes to Samantha, in want of feminine perspective.

She lifted her hands. "If you want your wife back, you're going to have to wage an effective campaign to win her heart."

Spoken like a true advertising executive, Will thought. Aware of how flawed her suggestion was, he chided, "Surely you're not suggesting Mr. Gentry advertise to get his wife back!"

Samantha gave Will a censoring look. "There is nothing wrong with that. Advertising is nothing more than communicating sentiments and feelings—as well as facts."

"Which is exactly what I need," Mr. Gentry exclaimed, ready to grab any lifeline thrown his way. "So, would you help me figure out how to do that where Mrs. Gentry is concerned?" the older gentleman asked Samantha.

She dipped her head. "Sure, in an informal kind of way. But I'm going to need a little time to think about the best approach."

Mr. Gentry thanked Samantha, told her where she could get in touch with him—at his fishing cabin on Lake Laramie, which unfortunately did not have a telephone—and left.

Will had wanted Samantha to become part of the Laramie community. He didn't want her doing anything that could conceivably cause bad feelings toward her later, should she decide to stay.

"Should you really have promised Mr. Gentry that?" Will asked mildly as soon as he and Samantha were alone.

She looked uneasy. "What do you mean?"

"Don't get me wrong." He shifted in his chair, struggling not to hurt her feelings. "Ad campaigns are effective sales tools."

"Yes," Samantha replied, clearly not liking the direction the conversation was headed. "They are."

Figuring this might go over better if the message was conveyed casually, Will moved around to sit on the front corner of his desk. "They are also often misleading in that they promise way more than can actually be delivered. I'd hate to see Mr. Gentry make his situation worse, which could happen if his wife thinks he is being the least bit superficial in his approach." Will paused, then tried again. "If Mrs. Gentry didn't like the card her husband got her…if that wasn't personal or specific enough…I don't see how any public campaign designed by a marketing professional could possibly provide a solution here."

Samantha's mouth quirked. "You don't think I can get them back together?" she taunted, rising gracefully from her chair. "Is that it?"

Will ignored the dark wavy hair spilling across one breast and focused on her face. "I think you're an amateur when it comes to decades-long marriages and relationships, yes. Just like I am," he admitted.

Samantha scoffed. "That's ridiculous," she muttered. Lips pursed in irritation, she slipped her notepad and pen back in her carryall.

"Huh?"

"Just because I don't have a boyfriend now doesn't mean I don't know what it would take for a guy to catch my eye."

He lifted a challenging brow. "And all women are interested in the same things, I suppose?"

Her slender shoulders stiffened at his deliberate misinterpretation of her pronouncement. "I didn't mean that and you know it, Will McCabe!"

Trying not to think how much he liked hearing her say his name, he slid off his desk to stand beside her. "Then what are you saying?" he asked, forcing himself not to think about what it would be like to hear her say his name—in ecstasy, not temper.

Oblivious to the lusty nature of his thoughts, she slid her carryall strap onto her shoulder and tucked the bag close to her side. "That I at least have some sensitivity in these matters."

He caught the implied dig. "And I don't—in your opinion?"

She merely smiled in a way that reminded him he had been the one who had given Mr. Gentry the poor advice.

"I know a lot about romance," Will declared irritably.

"Yeah?" Samantha tipped her chin in challenge. "Prove it!"

# Chapter Four

Samantha knew the moment the words were out of her mouth that she should never have thrown down the gauntlet.

Will gave her a slow, sexy smile. "Well, thank you, darlin'." He drew her carryall down her arm and tossed it aside. "I think I will."

She caught her breath and splayed her hands across the hard surface of his chest when he tugged her close. "I didn't mean on me!"

Ignoring her protest, he slid his hands through her hair, cupping her head, then started dropping kisses at her temple, along the curve of her cheekbone, the shell of her ear. "Ah, but what better subject to pepper with my subtle expertise."

He was enjoying this way too much—almost as much as she was. The air between them reverberated with excitement and escalating desire. Struggling to control her erratic breathing, Samantha decided that the only way to survive this would be by making light of the situation. Her cheeks burning, she retorted, "'Pepper' is right."

"Lucky for you," he whispered, holding her face steady when she tried to turn away. Then he rubbed his thumb across her lower lip, sensually tracing its shape. Eyes glinting mischievously, he brought her mouth up to his. "I like everything spicy—including my women."

*Not to mention his kisses*, Samantha thought. She trembled when his lips touched hers, causing her knees to go weak.

"This proves nothing," she murmured, arching against him as he took her lips in a kiss that was more intimate than anything she could have imagined. Stubbornly, she fought the riptide of sensations coursing throughout her body.

He dragged her so close they were almost one.

She closed her mouth, thinking that maybe—just maybe— if she kept the contact at a minimum, it wouldn't feel quite so erotic, so right, being with him this way.

But Will had other ideas. Pressing his hips against hers, he stopped kissing her long enough to lift his head. "Exactly why I've got to keep trying…."

And try he did, Samantha noted with a blissful sigh.

Gathering her closer still, he tilted his head and captured her lips with his. Once again she tried to resist, but the hot, sensual pressure of his mouth moving over hers was too intoxicating. Her heart beat wildly in her chest, and her head tipped back in surrender. His tongue swept inside her mouth, blazing a path that was as tender as it was fiery. Despite her decision to remain unaffected, yearnings she had pushed aside for far too long came rushing to the fore. It had been so long since she had been held, kissed, touched. Too long. And never like this—so gently and so masterfully.

He tasted so good, like man and sex and spice and everything that had always been missing in her life. He felt so hard and so strong, as capable of taking her as protecting her. Surrendering to the moment, Samantha parted her lips. Deepening the kiss, he soon had her rising up on tiptoe, wrapping her arms around his neck and pressing her breasts against his chest. And still he kissed her and held her, until she felt him straining against her, and she ached with wanting him, too.

Aware that she was suddenly in way over her head, knowing if they kept this up they could end up making hot, passionate love, Samantha came to her senses at long last. Trembling with a mixture of pleasure and shame, she shoved hard at his chest and stepped on his foot.

That got his attention.

Grimacing, he let her go. "Hint taken."

She glared at him. "You are incorrigible! You know that."

Will rubbed the back of his neck with the flat of his hand and studied her through narrowed eyes. Even now, he looked more up to the challenge than put off. "I've been called worse," he admitted with a shrug.

"That is not going to happen again."

He fixed her with a skeptical look. "If you say so."

Indignant, she retrieved her carryall and swung it back on her shoulder. "I do. Now if you don't mind, I have to go up and get ready for the meet-and-greet tonight. The town employees are hosting a party over at the Laramie Community Center, to wish Molly and my brother well in their betrothal." Everyone in town was invited. Molly really wanted Samantha to attend.

Interest lit Will's handsome face. "Want me to take you?"

"No thanks. I can drive myself."

Hoping he would cease and desist in his pursuit of her—at least for the moment—she gathered up her purchases and charged out of the office and up the stairs.

She stopped at the entrance to Will's private quarters. A second military-issue single bed and two canvas folding chairs had been brought into the room. Immediately, she was flooded with relief.

And something else, something she hadn't expected.

Disappointment?

Unwilling to let him know how comforting she had found his presence the night before, she murmured sarcastically, "At least you did something right."

Will had followed her up the stairs. Propping a hand on the

door frame, he gave her an impervious look. "So glad you approve."

She fiddled with her packages. "Now, if you don't mind…"

"No need to say more." He backed up, gave her another long, telling glance that had her knees going weak yet again. "I know how to make myself scarce."

"So one month's rent in New York City would pay for six months in an apartment here in Laramie," Samantha concluded, several hours later. She had half expected Will to show up at the event when the party began, if for no other reason than to torment her. He hadn't. And it was a shame, she thought, as she glanced around the room. It was one fine party, with a country and western band, a great Tex-Mex and barbecue spread, and lots of friendly townsfolk, including many of Will's relatives. It seemed, in these parts, there was no shortage of McCabes.

"Right," Lexie Remington McCabe said. The pregnant clothing designer took her husband's hand and smiled up at him.

Samantha noted the two of them exuded affection and made a beautiful couple. Watching them interact so lovingly—and Molly and Howard, and countless other couples in the big party room do the same—made Samantha feel a little envious. Although resigned to going it alone, she sometimes wished she had a mate who loved her even half as much. Someone to face life's challenges and joys with.

Not that Laramie, Texas, was without its drawbacks, she reminded herself fiercely, even if there did seem to be something in the air here that made people fall head over heels in love. "Of course salaries here are lower," she stated thoughtfully.

"Depends on what you do." Lewis helped himself to more guacamole from the buffet, then shared half of what he'd selected with his wife. "Because Lexie and I both own our own businesses, dealing with products that are marketed nation-wide, we actually net more than we would if we lived in California or New York, because our overhead—utilities, insurance, et cetera—are lower."

"We're not that far from Dallas-Fort Worth, Houston, San Antonio, even Austin." Lexie munched on a crispy tortilla chip. "All of which have tons of work for advertising agencies."

Samantha paused to think about that. It would be tough, getting started. On the other hand, she wouldn't have to worry so much about the nasty gossip Tippi Gallimore was spreading about her.

"Are you thinking about relocating here?" Lexie asked.

Samantha shrugged, adroitly sidestepping the question. "Molly's made it pretty clear she'd like it if I did."

Lexie chuckled. "Laramie has a great mayor in your future sister-in-law. She can't seem to stop selling the virtues of the area."

"Your brother, too," Lewis said.

"If there's anything I can do, any questions I can answer for you, don't hesitate to call," the designer said.

Her husband nodded. "Plenty of people around to help you if you decide to pick up stakes and move here."

That was another difference between rural Texas and the Big Apple, Samantha thought. The business in which she worked was extremely cutthroat and competitive in New York. At Gallimore, Smith & Tomberlin, backstabbing and professional sabotage were the norm. The seedy neighborhood in which she lived—all she could afford, what with the cost of living and her attempts to build a suitable wardrobe for work—did not foster the kind of Southern hospitality she had grown up with.

"Thanks." Samantha smiled.

"For what?" a familiar male voice asked behind her.

Samantha turned to face Will. He had shaved and showered and looked handsome as all get-out in a black Western shirt, jeans and boots. The black hat drawn low across his brow gave him a faintly dangerous look. He seemed more cowboy now than pilot.

"Mind if I steal this gal for a dance?" he asked, as soon as brief but affectionate greetings were exchanged.

"We were about to head out to the floor ourselves." Lewis took Lexie in his arms and two-stepped off.

Samantha's heartbeat kicked up a notch. Will's hands felt warm and possessive on her waist and palm as they started to dance. The ardent look in his eyes reminded her of their kiss.

Finding the memory a bit too arousing, she let her forehead rest against his shoulder. "I thought you weren't coming."

She sensed rather than saw his smile. "Missed me that much, huh?"

She drew a deep breath, straightened her spine. "I didn't miss you at all."

He let go of her hand long enough to rub his thumb across the curve of her cheek. Satisfaction gleamed in his blue eyes. "I can see that."

She wondered what had taken him so long to get there. Unexpected jealousy flared inside her. "Did you bring a date?" The impetuous words were out before she could stop them.

Looking almost insulted by the question, he tightened his grip on her. "If I had a date, I'd be dancing with her. The fact that I'm dancing with you…" he paused to touch his forehead to hers "…says I came alone. Just like you."

Samantha tried not to be too thrilled about that. And failed. It mattered, somehow, that she wasn't competing for his attention in that regard. At least not tonight.

Deciding she was allowing her thoughts and feelings to get much too personal where Will McCabe was concerned, she focused on the party. "Have you eaten yet? The buffet's wonderful," she exclaimed.

Will grinned, not the least dissuaded from his thoughts.

Moving her hair aside, he whispered in her ear, "You look good, too."

Just that quickly, he had her thinking about kissing him again.

"The difference is," she told him sternly, hoping to put an end to the teasing, "I'm not dinner."

"I'll try to keep that in mind."

When the dance ended, he gripped her hand possessively and led her toward the food tables.

"If you keep this up," Samantha murmured, aware of the curious glances they were getting, "people are going to think there's something between us."

"If I'm lucky, by the end of the week, there will be."

She looked up at the side of his face, and to her dismay, found him to be even more handsome in profile. She clamped her lips together. "Not funny, Will McCabe."

He let go of her hand and pressed a gallant palm to her spine. "Not supposed to be."

Aware that her pulse was racing, Samantha skidded to a stop at the end of the buffet. "You can't be hitting on me."

"I can't?" He looked like a kid who had just been caught raiding the cookie jar and didn't care.

"No," she countered. "You can't."

He merely smiled and seemed determined to prove her wrong. "Come on," he urged her genially. "You can show me what's good." While she tagged along, Will filled his plate to overflowing, then started toward the cloth-covered tables and chairs at one end of the room. He stopped abruptly. "On second thought…" He changed directions and tilted his head, indicating he wanted her to follow him.

Once she'd complied, he said, "There's someone I want you to meet." He led the way toward the community center kitchen. A petite white-haired woman with a Peter Pan haircut struggled with a nearly empty punch bowl and a large carton of sherbet. "Can I give you a hand with that, Mrs. Gentry?" Will asked. He set his filled dinner plate, silverware, napkin and drink down on the stainless steel counter, out of harm's way.

"Thank you, Will." The woman looked up at him gratefully. "It seems to be frozen solid."

"That it does. Maybe if we cut the carton away, instead of trying to spoon it out…" Will went to work. "By the way, this is Howard's little sister, Samantha. She's in advertising."

"Really." Yvonne Gentry perked up.

Yet another person who adored her older brother, Samantha thought.

"Mrs. Gentry was my English teacher my senior year at Laramie High School," Will continued.

"Now retired," Mrs. Gentry interjected.

"Married to Mr. Gentry, my high school physics teacher."

"Also retired, as of last June."

Will slid the sherbet into the punch bowl. "I couldn't have gotten through my senior year without them."

Mrs. Gentry carefully added two liters of ginger ale to the mix. "You were an excellent student at heart, especially when motivated."

Will lit up at the praise. "Mr. and Mrs. Gentry really knew how to inspire me, as well as every other kid that came into their classrooms."

Mrs. Gentry glowed. "Thank you, Will."

Samantha admired the mutual respect between him and his former teachers.

"Mr. Gentry here tonight?" Will asked casually.

The woman's attitude became chilly. She turned her back. "I wouldn't know."

Will picked up his dinner plate. "I realize it's none of my business."

Mrs. Gentry swung back around, lips pursed. "You're right about that," she scolded.

"But Oscar really loves you," Will insisted.

To no avail, Samantha noted.

The woman gave the punch a vigorous stir. "He needs better advice. Honestly, Will—" she propped one hand on her hip "—did you really think that flowers, perfume, candy and a card with sentiments written by someone else would fix everything?"

He shrugged, for the first time looking perplexed. "I hoped," he said.

"Well, you hoped wrong," Mrs. Gentry retorted irritably, shooing him on his way. "Do me a favor. Don't meddle again."

"Wow," Samantha murmured.

"She sure told me," Will agreed. Instead of going back into the community hall, where the band was still playing, he led the way out the fire doors, off the kitchen. More tables were set up on the sidewalk outside. Will selected one in a deserted area. Glad for a respite from the noise, music and bright lights, Samantha sank down in the chair he held out for her.

"Mr. Gentry must have done something pretty awful to make her so angry," she said, sipping her glass of mint-flavored iced punch.

Will settled close to her. "One would certainly think so. On the other hand, sometimes women get ticked off for no reason at all."

Samantha took another sip. "Speaking from experience, I gather?"

"As a matter of fact, I am." Will cut into his beef brisket and speared a piece with his fork. "My ex-wife divorced me with no warning, too."

No wonder he was so empathetic to Mr. Gentry's predicament, Samantha thought. Unable to quell her curiosity, she studied Will. "Surely your ex-wife said why."

Will nodded. "She considered me driven, rigid, inflexible, and more in love with flying than with her."

Samantha did a double take.

"What's ironic about it," Will continued affably, looking at her as if he wanted her to understand, "is that my ex knew I was in navy pilot training when we started dating. She knew I had an eight year commitment to the military ahead of me, that I would be gone for months at a time every year. We discussed it at length. She said it was fine. Then, during my very first deployment overseas, she decided it wasn't fine, after all, her on one side of the world, me on the other." He grimaced, remembering. "Next thing I know I'm getting papers served to me. By the time I learned about it, she already had a new boyfriend."

Samantha knew what it was like to be deserted by someone you loved and trusted and had thought you could rely upon to always be there for you. She reached over and touched his arm. "That's horrible," she said softly.

Will paused to reflect in a way that let her know he had long ago come to terms with what had happened. And that he'd forced himself to move on, as she hadn't.

"In retrospect, I see it was for the best," he told her quietly. "My ex and I never would have made it. She had this Hollywood idea of what life as an officer's wife was going to be like. Formal dances. Dress uniforms. Lots of glamour."

Samantha sat back and watched him break a roll in two. "And it turned out to be tough."

"Yes." Will spread butter on the roll with more care than necessary. "Lots of military spouses do it. They proudly run the home front while their husbands or wives are away, and warmly welcome them home when they return. I just picked the wrong gal."

"So you're not opposed to marriage." Samantha did not know why that would cheer her. Really, it was none of her business.

"Not at all." Will scooped up the last bit of barbecued brisket with his fork. He leaned back, savoring the dinner he had just inhaled with military efficiency. He paused to give Samantha a long, telling look. "I just need to be certain that the next woman in my life doesn't cut and run the minute the going gets a little tough." Appearing restless, he stood and took his dishes to the cart provided. "What about you?" he asked when he got back. He perched on the rock wall behind them instead of a chair. "You ever going to get married?"

"What makes you think I haven't been?" She quickly drained what was left of her tea and carried the empty glass over, too.

Will was still watching her when she returned to his side. "Have you been married?" he asked.

Resisting the urge to sit down beside him, Samantha stood restlessly in front of him. "No."

He regarded her intently. "Anyone ever ask?"

Someone had *promised* to do so. Remembering how she had been duped by the only man she'd ever opened up to, Samantha corralled her emotions. Aware that Will was still studying her in a way that made her body tingle, she looked toward the cars filling the parking lot and lining the streets. "Sore subject."

He caught her hand and pulled her down beside him on the rock wall, positioning her so her jean-clad thigh was pressed against his. "For the record," he said in a husky voice, "the bozo—whoever he was—is a fool."

Samantha looked at the way their hands were intertwined and resting on his leg. "Thanks."

"So…" Will tightened his grip. His eyes were full of understanding. "What are you looking for in a potential mate?"

This was all fantasy. She'd be leaving at the end of the week. Why not play along? "Oh, gosh." She withdrew her hand from the tantalizing warmth of his, telling herself it was okay to talk to her heart's content, even flirt a little, as long as she didn't let herself be vulnerable to more hurt and disappointment. "The list of qualifications is endless." She clasped her hands together on her lap.

Will studied her closely, looking as if he knew very well why she'd pulled away. "I've got time," he said.

*Make the qualifications sound impossible.*

"Well, he has to be smart," Samantha allowed grandly, crossing her legs at the knee. "And kind. Funny. Sweet. Sexy. Not too tall," she hastened to add, when it seemed that Will was mentally matching his own qualifications to her stated ones. "I don't want to date anyone, say, over seven feet. But—" she held up a cautioning finger "—he has to be tall enough that I can wear heels and not tower over him."

Will rubbed his jaw. "About my height," he drawled.

Samantha looked at him and pretended to find him wanting. "I guess your height would do."

The corners of his lips twitched at the exaggerated lack of enthusiasm in her voice. "I suppose he needs to be physically fit," he guessed.

Samantha moved her gaze away from the width of his shoulders and the solid musculature of his chest and abs. "Yes. But again, not *obsessed*. I don't want anyone who works out four hours a day or something like that, unless it was part of his job— if he were a professional athlete, for instance, or a ski instructor."

"Not likely to find either one of those around here," Will predicted sagely. "Since there's almost never any snow, no mountains to speak of and no gondolas, either. Nor are there any professional sports teams of any kind."

*You got that not-too-subtle point, did you?* Samantha flashed a sardonic smile. "Also, he cannot like rap music."

Will hesitated, as if this could be a problem. Which she was sure was not a difficulty for him, since she knew his truck radio was tuned to a country and western station.

"Seriously." He made a good show of looking disappointed. "No rap?"

Samantha shook her head. "Not a measure of it. I've heard far too much of it blaring on the streets of New York City at 3:00 a.m. to want to ever listen to it again."

He dipped his head in mocking acknowledgment. "I see your point."

"I can deal with all kinds of music, as long as it's *music*," Samantha continued.

He regarded her eagerly. "Then the Lawrence Welk orchestra would be okay?"

Samantha giggled despite herself. She didn't know anyone their age who was that retro. "Funny."

"I thought so."

"Actually," she confessed, "orchestra music of that style is a little old-fashioned for me."

"Me, too."

Silence fell, and their eyes met. Samantha felt an intimacy she didn't expect welling up between them. Will looked a little taken aback, too.

"How about karaoke?" he suggested finally, picking up the banter where they'd left off.

Samantha made a face. She could do a lot of things, but singing—in the right key, anyway—was not one of them. Not about to show him any weakness, she merely shrugged. "I'd have to be drinking margaritas."

He caught a strand of her hair and tucked it behind her ear. "You're cute when you smile."

*You're dangerous when you make me laugh.* Her insides fluttering, Samantha drew in a breath. "I hope you're not hitting on me again."

"Me? Wouldn't think of it," he declared with a smirk. He aimed a thumb at the center of his chest. "I know the rules."

"You better," she warned.

He nudged her lightly. "Not that there are any rules against *you* hitting on *me*."

She stood and parodied her most kick-butt stance. "We're not going to need any."

He widened his knees and tugged her between his spread legs. "Sure about that?" he teased.

The back of her knee bumped the inside of his rock-hard thigh.

"It's not going to happen," she insisted, trembling at the point of contact.

He gave her a slow smile that indicated he was a very patient, very thorough lover. The implication caused her to shiver all over.

His fingers stroked the inside of her wrist. "Want to bet?"

Figuring it would be a sign of weakness if she were to pull away, she stated firmly, "I don't gamble on love—er, sex."

Obviously enjoying how flustered she'd become, Will leaned back thoughtfully. "Exactly the problem, up till now."

She clamped her lips together, telling herself it was one thing to flirt, another to tear down the barriers and make love. "You're not going to change my mind," she insisted.

His brows shot up. "I know *you* think that."

With her breathing not nearly as deep or even as she would like, she stepped back. Averting her glance away from his obvious arousal, she said, "Being in Laramie is not going to change me."

He rose slowly, the picture of masculine grace. Serious now, he reiterated quietly, "I know you think that, too."

Just that quickly, Samantha could see the two of them in bed, bodies locked together in perfect harmony. With effort, she shut out the image of her beneath him. What did it matter if she fantasized about making love with him, just a bit? It wasn't going to happen. Any more than her staying here permanently was going to happen. She swallowed around the parched feeling in her throat. "Yet you're convinced otherwise."

He took her chin between his fingers and kissed her mouth, confidence radiating from him. "Some things, I just know."

# Chapter Five

"There's a message for you," Will told Samantha the next morning, when she walked into his office.

"On your voice mail?" Samantha tried not to notice how good he looked, even in a sweat-dampened T-shirt and running shorts. That must have been some workout he'd had. She wondered just how far and fast he'd run, and if he was struggling against the same temptations as she.

Obviously in need of replenishment after his workout, Will guzzled half a bottle of water, wiped his mouth with the back of his hand, then used the neck of his navy T-shirt to blot the moisture from his face. "Guess you forgot to give Oscar Gentry your cell phone number," he said.

"I'll do that right now," Samantha promised. She took her phone out into the hall and called Oscar back, to discover he was on his way over to see her, and would arrive within the half hour.

Will met her at the door to his office, a hand towel looped around his neck. "There's coffee, juice and fresh buttermilk biscuits for the staff in the break room on the other side of the hangar." He headed for the stairs that led to his private quarters. "You can help yourself," he said over his shoulder.

"Thanks." Samantha crossed the hangar, greeting the other pilots and maintenance men as she went.

Jets had been taking off since dawn. Others were getting

fueled up and ready to go. It was business as usual at McCabe Charter Jet Service. Consequently, she had the anonymity she craved. Instead of being relieved that the week before her brother's wedding would likely pass much faster than she had expected, she felt...let down. Part of it was that the evening before had ended on such an unexpectedly dull note. She had figured Will would try to put the moves on her—at least work in a good-night kiss—when they got back to the airstrip. Instead, he had called it a night and retreated to his office.

With a perplexed sigh, Samantha grabbed some breakfast and headed back to Will's office. She had just finished eating when Oscar Gentry walked in. She rose and extended a hand. "May I offer you some breakfast?"

"No thanks." He settled in a chair opposite her. "I want to get down to business. What have you planned for me so far by way of an advertising campaign?"

Samantha sat back down, too, knowing this wasn't going to be easy for him to hear. "I met your wife last evening."

"I was with her." Will walked in, freshly showered, clad in black uniform trousers and a starched white shirt. He sent his old teacher an empathetic look. "I think I should be honest. You wife still seemed pretty ticked off at me and you!"

Oscar grimaced. "Exactly why I need an advertising campaign."

Samantha held up a cautioning hand. "I have to tell you, Mr. Gentry. After speaking with your wife last night, I don't think doing anything big or ostentatious is the way to win her back."

His face fell. "Why not?"

"Because it's likely to make her feel pressured, more in the public eye than she already is regarding your separate living arrangements," Samantha explained. "This would likely cause more talk. More interference. She's not going to respond well to more people meddling in what she considers a private marital difficulty."

Oscar frowned, the picture of abject misery. He clasped both hands behind his neck. "Did she tell either of you why she's upset with me?"

When Will and Samantha both shook their heads, he exhaled slowly and dropped his hands to his lap. "Then how am I going to win Yvonne back?" he asked, looking more discouraged than ever.

"I think you're going to have to start at square one," Samantha advised, deciding a practical but heartfelt approach was best. "Go back to the beginning and woo her the way you did when you were courting her. You know *that* worked."

Mr. Gentry began to look excited. "You mean, throw pebbles at her window, serenade her, ask her to go out on a date with me?"

Samantha nodded in encouragement. "If that is what worked to get her attention before, then yes. Women love persistence."

Will started to grin, obviously reading way too much into what she'd said. Samantha scowled and met his gaze. "I'm not talking about you."

He made no effort to stifle a cheeky grin, but gave her an amused once-over. "That sounded like a general rule to me."

Samantha tingled in every place his eyes had touched and some places they hadn't. With effort, she pushed the desire away. "It is." She paused to let her words sink in. "For every man in Texas but you."

Mr. Gentry blinked, perplexed. He jerked a thumb at Will. "Why is he excluded?"

"Because," Samantha said, ignoring the ornery smile playing at the corners of Will's mouth, "he falls into the category of annoying men. When an annoying man is persistent, it only makes the woman madder, and less likely to go out with him."

Will cleared his throat but made no comment.

Sure she'd made her point, Samantha went on counseling

the lovelorn retiree. "I am sure, if you remind Mrs. Gentry of why she fell in love with you in the first place, she will start to fall for you all over again."

Hope warred with apprehension in the older man's eyes. "If this doesn't work…"

"It will. You've got to feel confident of that. That's another thing women love. Confidence in a man. Again—" Samantha looked at Will before he could throw in his two cents' worth of bad advice "—I am not talking about you."

Will regarded her with mock solemnity. He touched two fingers to his brow. "Got you."

Appearing oblivious to the tension between the two younger people in the room, Mr. Gentry mused out loud, "I guess I could start with the pebble throwing tonight. Maybe take my guitar and serenade her…."

"Now you're talking," Samantha enthused. "You know, she really does love you."

Will rocked back on his heels, looking surprised once again. Obviously, Samantha thought, he did not consider her a romantic person.

And the truth was, usually she wasn't. Normally, she considered all the hearts and flowers stuff a bunch of nonsense. But something about being back in the heart of Texas was altering her cynical nature. Had her appreciating the beauty of damn near everything, and hoping for miracles. Hoping that once again love—and family—would prevail.

"And you can tell my wife loves me because…?" Mr. Gentry persisted.

Samantha stood and came over to pat his hand. "Mrs. Gentry is so all-fired worked up about whatever it is you did or didn't do for her. If she really didn't care, she'd be apathetic. She's not."

Oscar offered a weak smile, standing in turn. "You're right about that," he admitted, a tad more hopefully. "Yvonne is pretty hot under the collar." He drew an enervating breath. "I'll just have to give it my all."

"Keep me posted on how it's going," Samantha said.

"I will." Mr. Gentry promised.

Silence fell in the office after the older gentleman thanked her and left. Will sat down at his desk and checked his e-mail for any new messages.

Samantha turned to him, hands on her hips. "I can't believe you have nothing to say."

He flashed her a satisfied smile, the kind that said he would challenge her views in his own way, in his own time. "Do you want to check your e-mail—via the Web?"

Not exactly the repartee she'd been expecting, but a good idea, nevertheless. Especially if it kept her mind off him.

Samantha retreated into scrupulous politeness. "Actually, I would, if you don't mind." She sat down at the computer, quickly went to Web mail and zipped through her messages.

Will looked up from the stack of paperwork he'd been perusing when she let out a heavy sigh. "Bad news?"

"More rejection," she admitted reluctantly. Via form letter, sent out electronically, no less.

Will wrote across the top of a paper in red pen, then flipped to the next page. "Do you still have résumés out?"

Despite her sinking spirits, Samantha managed a nod. "A couple. One in particular—Blount & Levine—holds some promise." She smiled at the question in his eyes. "It's my old firm's top rival. They sat on my request for a job interview for months, then asked me for sample ad copy, college transcripts and references a few weeks ago—and then…nothing."

His gaze reflected the kind of hope she wished she could feel. "Maybe they'll still come through with an interview."

Wistfulness swept through her as she thought about what it might be like to have a man like Will cheering her on from the sidelines. "I hope so." She regarded him gratefully. "If they do,

I'll have to give it all I've got. It's about my only option left in the New York City area."

"Meantime, you've got the work here," he said encouragingly.

Samantha sank back in his swivel chair, glad to have something besides her own travails to focus on. "Speaking of which…I did a preliminary study of the data you gave me—"

"That's good," Will interrupted, making another mark and flipping to yet another page. "But I already know exactly what I want in an advertising campaign."

Clients like this—who refused to let you do your job— were the worst, Samantha thought.

"I want you to convince business travelers who book with my jet service to start returning home on Saturday, or heading out on Sunday."

Samantha had already noticed that Will's airlines had fifty percent less business on weekends. "Your heavy booking days are Monday and Friday."

"Right. There's a slight dropoff on Tuesday, Wednesday and Thursday, but the biggest hit we take is on weekends. And that is when a couple of my part-timers are able to take on more flights."

Samantha pondered that briefly. "I see your point," she responded evenly. "But I'd still like to present you with some alternate ways to go." His approach was so narrow, it wouldn't accomplish much. If he'd just let her get a word in edgewise, she could explain why.

He regarded her with barely masked impatience. "Let's not make this more complicated than it needs to be. All I want are print ads for the major Texas city newspapers."

Deciding it best not to alienate him completely, she asked carefully, "What's the budget?"

He named a figure that was woefully small, given the financial return he wanted to realize.

He dropped the papers in the basket on his desk and sat

down next to her. "How soon could you have mock-ups ready for me to look at?"

Samantha calculated how long it would take to make him see he was making a huge mistake by not allowing her to fully exercise her creative powers. "Later today."

Will glanced at his watch. "Actually, tomorrow will be soon enough," he told her in a businesslike tone, "since I've got a flight and won't be back until seven or eight this evening."

Before Samantha could reply, Howard strolled in. "I was hoping you'd be here," her brother said. "I'd like to take you to see my new office in town." Stuffing his hands in the pockets of his slacks, Howard continued casually, "I thought maybe the two of us could go to lunch." He searched her eyes for any sign of warmth. "Have some time alone to catch up."

"Thanks." It was hard to feel anything but manipulated under the circumstances. "But I'm working on an ad campaign for Will," she said coolly.

Will gave her a sharp look. "I'm not in that much of a rush for the new ads." He made a shooing gesture toward the door. "Go and spend time with your brother."

Now she knew it was a setup.

"*You* go spend time with him." Samantha got up and stalked out of the office. Over her shoulder, she said to Howard, "Next time call first. You'll save yourself a trip."

She heard muted voices behind her—some sort of man-to-man discussion she was tempted to stay and eavesdrop on. However, not wanting either of them to have a chance to say anything else to her again, she walked outside, past the centrally located observation tower and deck.

During the break room chatter that morning, she had learned that noted industrialist Jake Remington, filmmaker Beau Chamberlain and multimillionaire oilman Wade McCabe all had personal jets housed in private hangars on airstrip property. Samantha strolled down to look at them and tried not to fume.

Only when she saw her brother's Mercedes leave the property did she saunter back to the quartet of hangars that comprised McCabe Charter Jet Service.

Will was still in his office. Another guy in uniform she recognized as Will's copilot strolled in. "You about ready to go?" he asked Will.

He gave a terse nod. "I'll meet you out at the plane in five."

Will opened a tall metal locker in the corner, withdrew a black leather aviator jacket, tie and pilot's hat. He looked at Samantha but didn't say anything. His silence was killing her, especially since she knew darn well what he was thinking. "What?" she blurted sweetly. "No lecture about me turning down my brother's invitation to lunch?"

"Hey." He pushed up the brim of his hat and shrugged. "If you're okay turning down a free meal—you being unemployed and all—who am I to judge?"

She glared at him. "Low blow, McCabe."

He regarded her with disapproval. "So is your repeated dissing of your brother." He continued to study her as if trying to figure out the answer to a puzzle. "At what point do you think you will have punished him enough?" he asked softly.

That was just it, Samantha thought dismally, watching Will head for the aircraft. She didn't know.

WILL HAD PROMISED Howard he would handle his friend's kid sister during her stay in Laramie. Thus far, he wasn't exactly doing a bang-up job of softening Samantha up. Will supposed on one level that was no surprise. Manipulating someone else into behaving a certain way was not really his thing. He preferred to live and let live, unless the person in question was deliberately hurting others. Then, he had a hard time standing by, doing and saying nothing. Instinct made him want to step in, take charge, make everyone behave according to protocol.

Not that restoring the peace was always easy. It wasn't like business, where he could simply fire someone who proved to be a liability rather than an asset. Family situations were much more complicated. They required a delicate hand he wasn't certain he always had. Especially in the case of the very complicated and sexy Samantha Holmes.

Not that she would be his problem for long, since she was planning to hightail it out of Laramie the minute the wedding was over. Unless someone…namely him…was able to talk sense into her and make her see what she'd be giving up.

Had Will not owed Howard so much, he might have said to heck with peacemaking, and thrown in the towel. He couldn't do that. Not in good conscience. So the moment he arrived back in Laramie, said goodbye to his copilot and turned the plane over to the mechanic for the postflight inspection, he headed for his hangar office.

Samantha was right where he had expected her to be, seated at his desk, bent over a sketch pad with a frown on her face.

"Shouldn't you be at the backyard barbecue tonight at Molly's?" he asked, knowing practically anyone would have been better at getting her to cooperate than him.

Samantha's pretty chin took on that familiar, stubborn tilt. "The meet-and-greet for out-of-town bridesmaids and groomsmen was optional."

Will folded his arms across his chest and waited. Her next excuse wasn't long in coming.

"Molly understands I'm working."

The time for cordial persuading had passed.

"You're going if I have to throw you over my shoulder and haul you there like a sack of potatoes," Will warned.

Samantha scoffed until she saw how serious he was. "You wouldn't dare."

Trying not to think how much fun that might actually be,

he gave her a speculative look and promised. "On the contrary, I consider it my duty as best man to see that you—the maid of honor—is there."

THE THREAT ECHOING in her ears, Samantha watched Will hang up his jacket and tie, put his hat on the shelf and head up the stairs.

Thinking the unexpected maelstrom was over, she went back to her sketching of the sample ad.

Three minutes later he was back—in civilian clothes. Radiating a kind of resolve that made her mouth go dry, he perused her from head to toe, taking in her boot-cut black jeans, sparkly black tank top and black Western shirt. "Good thing it's casual."

Knowing they had some very important boundaries to set, she clutched her sketch pad in front of her like a shield. "You cannot be serious."

Looking very much the maverick ex-military man, he studied her with shuttered eyes and murmured complacently, "If you think that, you don't know me at all."

Trying not to think how handsome he looked, she squirmed and muttered, "Howard had no right to tell you about my childhood."

"I gather you're talking about the way you behaved when people tried to adopt you?"

Samantha drew a deep breath and clenched her teeth. "I don't know what is so hard to understand about that. I didn't want to be part of someone else's family!"

"Clearly."

Figuring there was no time better than the present to state her feelings on her brother's actions, she said, "Howard never should have terminated his familial rights and given his okay for me to be adopted by the first family that came down the pike and showed an interest."

To Samantha's surprise, Will didn't argue that her brother's approach hadn't been devastating to her emotionally. "Yeah, well," he said after a moment, "Howard's sorry for that now."

Words, Samantha thought, were cheap.

"But maybe he's not." She tried to step past, only to find her way blocked. "Maybe Howard just wants to try to look good in Molly's eyes."

Sensing—correctly—that she was about to dart the other way, Will caught her hand. "He's trying his darnedest to make it up to you and meet you halfway."

"Wrong. He's just trying to save face in front of Molly and all his new friends."

"You really don't know your brother at all, do you?" Will groused.

"And you do?"

"Better than you, apparently!" Will frowned, letting go of her hand. "Otherwise you wouldn't be so afraid to go tonight."

"I'm not afraid."

"Prove it."

Samantha stared at Will.

Will stared back.

"Fine." Sketchpad still clutched to her chest, she stalked past him and out to his pickup truck.

They put on their safety belts in tense silence.

Will started the engine and drove off. After a while, he said in a much more conciliatory tone, "Look, Samantha, I'm sorry you grew up without a family, but you have to take at least partial responsibility for that, since, initially anyway, there were families interested in adopting you."

"If they had chosen me," Samantha said wearily, the crushing pain coming back to the forefront, as she turned her gaze to the passing scenery.

Cattle stood together in groups in the moonlight. Horses roamed along the fences. The occasional oil well moved in slow, steady rhythm, bringing crude out of the ground. She saw well-lit ranch houses of all shapes and sizes. Churches and schools.

"There was no guarantee anyone who came to the monthly sessions arranged by social services, for kids and would-be parents, would have gone in my favor," she said as Will drove through the outskirts of town.

Even through the semidarkness of the cab, she could see Will found that bit of news incredible.

"What are you talking about?" he demanded. "Howard showed me a photo of you when you were eight. You were every bit as gorgeous then as you are now." He cast an admiring look her way. "Not to mention precocious as hell, from the sounds of it. You were exactly what most adoptive parents are looking for."

Aware that Will made her feel beautiful in a way no one else ever had, Samantha pulled her bent leg up on the seat. "That's not the way I saw it," she responded glumly. Turning her face away from him, she rested her cheek on her knee. "Howard hadn't wanted me in his life," she recounted bitterly. "He hadn't wanted to take care of me, and he was my brother—we were all the family each other had!"

"So you concluded nobody else would want you, either," Will guessed in a voice that sounded as raw around the edges as she felt.

Samantha turned to look at him again. She said in a low tone laced with regret, "I only had to go to one of those events and see how devastated all the kids were after they weren't matched up with anyone to know that kind of cattle-call rejection wasn't for me."

He looked at her, understanding in his eyes. "So you acted out."

She leaned back in her seat, not ashamed to admit it. "Every chance I got, you're darn right I did."

Telling herself she hadn't wanted another family, anyway, had been her only protection against the vicious cycle of hope and rejection. It had been easier simply to harden her heart against further hurt.

Will turned his attention back to the road. "Still, some people selected you anyway."

Aware that they had reached the center of town, Samantha nodded slowly. "I was taken home with a family a few times. It wasn't long before I was sent back to the group home. But unlike the other kids who got rejected, I didn't cry over it," she said in a voice drained of all sorrow—and hope. "Just like I'm not crying now."

"Except you do cry," Will accused quietly. He steered the truck into an empty lot in front of a store that had long since closed, and put the engine in Park. "Every night. In your sleep."

# Chapter Six

Will studied Samantha's anguished expression. She looked both older and younger than her years. Color seeped into her cheeks, even as the rest of her paled. There were shadows beneath her dark brown eyes that hadn't been there the night they'd met in New York City, and he knew he was partially responsible for putting them there. A mixture of guilt and remorse swept through him, prompting him to act. Cutting the engine, he released his seat belt and eased across the bench seat to her side.

"What do you mean, I cry every night in my sleep?" she echoed warily.

He wrapped his arms around her and eased her against him protectively. The fragrance of her hair and skin filled his senses. His eyes lingered on the soft, erratic rise and fall of her breasts. "No one's ever told you that before?"

Abruptly, some of the light left her eyes and her face looked tense and anxious. "It used to happen when I was a kid," she muttered, glancing away.

"When did it stop?" he asked her gently.

She shrugged, looking even more uncomfortable.

Unable to help himself, he reached out to touch her cheek. As he felt the softness of her skin once again, another jolt of desire swept through him. "You don't really know, do you?"

She leaned into his touch for one millisecond before drawing away. "How would I know one way or another, since I never wake up when I am crying—unless someone wakes me up?" She rubbed a thumb over her jean-clad knee.

He continued holding her, and after a moment, she went on. "The psychologist I saw when I was a kid said it was a symptom of stress." Her teeth raked across her lower lip. "Given the fact I'm currently unemployed and having a heck of a time finding another position, and dealing with you and my brother, it's no wonder I'm feeling stressed." Turning away, she eased out of his embrace and looked at her watch. "If we don't get a move on we'll miss the entire party. Not that this bothers me, but…"

Ignoring his instinct—which was to pull Samantha back into his arms and hold her close until the hurt she had suffered went away—Will restarted the engine, put the truck in gear and drove on. He wanted to broach this with Samantha again, but at a more appropriate time. Maybe even run her symptoms by his stepmom, since Kate was a psychologist who specialized in grief counseling. Samantha was still clearly grieving.

Samantha remained silent while Will navigated the scant evening traffic in the center of town. Short minutes later, they reached Molly's home. Cars lined the streets. It was clear from the sounds of music and laughter pouring out of the residence that the party was still in full swing.

Samantha left her sketch pad and pencil on the seat and headed up the walk with him. "I hope you're happy now," she muttered, climbing the steps.

He wouldn't be happy until she had put all her demons to rest. Will sensed she knew that, too.

He caught her hand and squeezed. "You're doing the right thing, coming here tonight."

Samantha rolled her eyes and punched the doorbell.

Molly opened the door and quickly embraced them each in

a hug. "I'm so glad you were able to come!" Exuberant as ever, she waved them in. "Will, you already know everyone here, so make yourself at home." She then linked arms with Samantha. "I'm going to introduce you around."

Without a backward glance, Samantha headed off with her.

Will's stomach rumbled, reminding him it had been hours since he had eaten. He made his way to the buffet, where Howard joined him. "You made my day, buddy," his friend said, slapping Will on the back. "Getting her here."

*Under protest.*

"No problem," Will said, figuring what Howard didn't know wouldn't hurt him in this case.

His friend regarded him in awe. "I didn't think it was possible to soften my little sis up, but everything you've done, from providing her a place to bunk while she's in town to making up some advertising work for her to do…"

Will smiled and nodded at the Nedermeyers, who were chatting with Samantha and Molly across the room.

"I didn't make up work," Will corrected. "I actually do need some help."

"The point is," Howard stated, "the task you gave her has engaged Samantha enough to keep her from bolting."

Perhaps not for long, Will thought. He looked at his friend. "You still have a lot of work to do to make amends," he reminded him.

"I'm going to," Howard promised, glancing over at Samantha, who was still engaged in lively conversation with the Nedermeyers. "I'll even make another attempt tonight," he continued, "if you can keep Samantha around after everyone leaves."

"I'll see what I can do," Will promised, knowing what he needed was a way to break the ice between Samantha and her brother, just get them talking. After thinking about it a few minutes longer, he figured out a way.

Thanks to Molly, by the time the guests left an hour later, Will figured Samantha had met everyone at the gathering. She'd appeared to be having a good time, so long as her brother stayed away from her. To Will's chagrin, every time Howard approached, Samantha had visibly tensed. Taking the hint, Howard had busied himself elsewhere during the rest of the party, as had Will. Now, with the festivities dwindling rapidly, it was time to fish or cut bait. A fact Samantha apparently knew, too. She walked over to Will and looked him in the eye.

"I'm really tired," she said.

She didn't appear tired, Will noted. She looked ready to run.

Not about to fail his friend if he could help it, Will put the second part of his plan for the evening in action. "Your brother wants to see the ad campaign you've been working on for me."

Will figured that had to be true, even if Howard hadn't actually come out and said as much.

"I'd love to see it, too," Molly exclaimed, walking up to join them.

Will looked at Samantha with a challenging smile. "What do you say? Are you up to doing a pitch for them, too?" He paused deliberately, met her eyes. "Or would that be too much pressure?"

As expected, his taunt raised her hackles in no time.

Samantha glared at him, then continued smoothly, "I'd be delighted to get their input on the concept you've had me working on. All I need is my sketch pad from the truck."

"I'll get it," Howard offered quickly, knowing a golden opportunity when he saw one.

By the time her brother returned, Samantha had Molly and Will seated on the sofa. She encouraged Howard to join them, then turned to the appropriate sketch.

"The first ad starts with the caption, 'Why hurry home?' At the bottom of the page it says, 'Saturday is soon enough to get there.' The photo in the middle shows everything the harried businessperson is avoiding—laundry piled sky-high, grass in need of cutting, bills to pay.

"The second ad says, 'Can't wait to get back to work?' Then it shows a photo of a packed business calendar and follows with the slogan, 'McCabe Charter Jet Service can fly you there faster.' At the corner of both ads is the company logo, 24–7, every week." Samantha looked at Will. "I don't know if that's true or not, but if there are days you don't fly at all, we can asterisk it at the bottom of the ad in tiny letters. Something like 'Except Christmas and New Year's Day' or whatever."

"Very clever," Will said.

"I agree," Howard declared enthusiastically.

"Except…" Molly frowned, looking reluctant to continue.

"It's a little dull, isn't it?" Samantha stated matter-of-factly.

Will studied her, realizing too late that he had shortchanged her by simply telling her what to do, instead of outlining the problem and letting her creativity and experience take wing.

"I suppose you have another idea?" he said.

Samantha beamed, looking as if she had been waiting an entire lifetime for him to ask. "As a matter of fact…" She smiled and turned the page of her sketch pad. "I did come up with another approach, one that I feel is much more on target with your core audience."

*Of course*, Will thought.

"Your company caters to the traveling adult, not families," Samantha explained.

"Right."

"But the bookings don't all have to be customers on business trips, particularly on weekends—and midweek— where you are trying to increase sales."

"I'm with you," Will said, noting that Molly and Howard looked equally intrigued.

"I suggest you try and partner with upscale golf resorts in temperate climates, not within easy driving distance of Texas,"

Samantha continued. "Places you'd have to fly. Advertise in the sports pages, next to the golf news under the caption 'Affordable Luxury.' Show a group of guys with their clubs boarding one of your jets, and then split the ad to show them at the resort, ready to play on a beautiful green."

Picking up steam as she went, Samantha flipped to her next drawing. "Do the same thing in the lifestyle section for women," she suggested. "Partner with a spa. Run the caption, 'Pamper Yourself,' and show a group of female friends boarding a McCabe charter, and then getting relaxing massages." She waited while everyone took a good look at the sketched sample ad. "You'd have the McCabe Charter Jet Service logo worked into every ad, here in the upper right-hand corner, with the invitation to call for rates and vacation packages."

"Wow," Molly said.

"That is amazing," Howard agreed.

Samantha looked at Will, her cheeks pink with excitement.

He didn't have to feign anything; he was sincerely impressed. "You beat my idea by a Texas mile." He stood. "Congratulations." He closed the distance between them and shook her hand. "You just earned a permanent place on my payroll."

SAMANTHA COULDN'T HELP IT—she was still glowing as she and Will said good-night to Howard and Molly and headed out to his pickup truck. She couldn't say why she was so elated. She routinely did great work and was praised for it. Yet something about Will's appreciation warmed her inside and out in a way no one else's ever had. And he seemed pretty happy, too. Happier than the situation would seem to indicate.

"We'll talk money tomorrow, either in person or through our lawyers, however you're comfortable," Will promised, sliding his hand beneath her elbow as they navigated the slightly uneven surfaces of the sidewalk.

He paused to unlock his truck doors with the remote keypad in his hand. "I want you under contract for this as soon as possible."

Samantha knew she had every right to accept payment and could really use the money. Yet, nonsensical as it was, she didn't want money changing hands between them. She didn't want their relationship moving from budding friendship on the threshold of romance, to something more predictable and confining.

She brought her sketch pad up to her chest and held it in front of her like a shield of armor. The streetlamps cast a golden glow over them, making the moment all the more surreal.

"I owe you a favor, remember?" she said softly.

He dismissed her attempt to keep the situation strictly personal.

"You more than fulfilled your room-and-board obligation with those great ideas." He held the door for her. When she had settled on the bench seat, he propped a boot on the sill of the passenger door and leaned in. "I want a real business deal for us. In fact—" he paused, scanning her face "—I'd like to see if you can't find some resorts interested and pitch to them yourself."

What could she say to that? It was an opportunity to add to her résumé and expand her business contacts. "Okay." Samantha struggled with her safety belt.

Will reached in to unsnarl the belt where it had twisted. When he handed it over, his fingers brushed hers and lingered. Her heartbeat accelerated all the more.

"You really are talented." He gazed at her closely.

Samantha swallowed. "Thanks."

They exchanged smiles.

Will headed for the driver's seat. A comfortable silence fell as he guided his pickup onto the street.

"Did you enjoy yourself this evening?" he asked eventually.

"Yes." She fingered the spiral binder of her sketch pad, aware the friendly hospitality of the town was wearing off on her, making her feel quite at home. Will McCabe was doing the same.

"I even found a way to pick up some extra cash while I'm in town, starting the day after tomorrow," she confided.

"What are you talking about?" Will sent her a curious glance.

Houses grew sparse as they left town. Samantha smiled at a herd of cattle, standing together in a semicircle, the moonlight reflecting off their speckled white-and-rust coats.

"The Nedermeyers need someone to water their houseplants and take care of their backyard pets twice a day through Saturday noon." Aware she was babbling, yet unable to help herself, Samantha continued on, "Apparently, 'the kids' are older and don't require much, just someone looking in on them and making sure they have everything they need. I said I'd do it for them." Samantha paused. "Why are you looking at me like that?"

Will shrugged, appearing more than a little baffled by her actions. He continued driving. "I just never figured you for the type that would take on that particular kind of responsibility," he said.

"Hey!" She angled a thumb at her sternum, "I need the money. As far as I'm concerned, work is work."

Will exhaled slowly, then murmured, "I hope you don't live to regret it."

What was there to regret when her meager efforts would yield her some much-needed cash? Samantha wondered.

Will didn't illuminate further. They were still silent when he parked in the airstrip lot once again.

"Mind if I check my e-mail before I go to bed?" Samantha asked when they walked into the hangar.

"Help yourself," Will said. He booted up his computer,

brought up the Internet, then offered the desk to her. Samantha scrolled through her messages, expecting only more bad news or no news. For once, she was wrong about what was coming. As she read, her face split in a wide grin. "Way to go me!" she cheered excitedly, practically leaping out of her chair. Will arched a brow in silent inquiry. She explained, "One of the execs at Blount & Levine wants to meet with me tomorrow at 3:00 p.m. for a job interview!"

WILL HAD PROMISED he would take her back to New York if she got a job interview, and he was as good as his word, Samantha discovered. He even went so far as to reschedule several of his pilots so he would be free to fly her there himself early the following morning.

Once they'd landed, they raced to her apartment. Samantha hurriedly showered, dressed in a white Armani pant suit that had cost more than a month's rent on her studio apartment, and gathered up her portfolio. She called for a cab, then began to pace. Will pointed to the blinking light on her answering machine. "You've got twenty-seven messages."

He wasn't kidding. "Keep an eye out for the cab while I listen," Samantha said.

"Sure." Will stood sentry at the window overlooking the street.

The first five or six were nothing—two telemarketers, her landlord, friends wanting to know if she wanted to take in the new exhibit at the Metropolitan. The rest were of a different caliber. "Samantha, hi, it's Glinda. Call me back." Five or six more of the same, and then Glinda whispered into the phone, "Listen, I don't know where you are, but you've got to be warned. Tippi Gallimore somehow found out you're being considered for a position at Blount & Levine and she is on the warpath!"

"Who is Tippi Gallimore?" Will asked.

Samantha could feel the blood draining from her face. "The vindictive wife of Shawn Gallimore."

Still keeping an eye out, Will moved closer. "What has she got against you?"

Samantha caught a flash of yellow on the street. "I don't have time to get into it right now." She rushed toward the door.

"Hey," Will said.

Samantha turned at the portal.

"Good luck."

She took a deep breath. "Thanks." She was going to need it.

Luckily, the rest of her afternoon went smoothly. Samantha felt much more confident by the time she got back to her apartment, shortly after seven that evening, and found Will relaxing on her sofa, reading a book.

"So how was the interview?" he asked.

Trying not to think how it might feel to have him here waiting for her for more than just today, Samantha dropped her portfolio and shoulder bag onto the coffee table. "Great." Exhausted, she perched on the arm of the sofa next to him, took off her heels and rubbed her aching feet. "I talked to a total of six people. They all really liked some of the campaigns I've worked on so far."

He reached over to swing her legs onto his lap. His massaging hands worked magic on her arches. "Think you'll get the job?"

She had to work not to groan in ecstasy, his touch was that soothing. "I don't know."

"Tippi Gallimore?" He worked his way up the tense muscles of her calves.

Aware she'd be a puddle of relaxed nerve endings if he continued, Samantha withdrew her legs from his tender ministrations and stood. She padded barefoot over to her closet, grabbed a cotton sweater and jeans, and disappeared behind the bathroom door. "You're not going to let that drop, are you?" she said, around the barrier.

"Not when it is clearly upsetting you, no." His voice was low and determined.

Samantha finished changing and came back out to hang her most expensive business suit on a padded hanger.

Will was still watching her. Knowing she needed to unburden herself, and realizing Will was a very good listener, she walked to the fridge and brought back two bottles of diet soda. She handed one to him and sat down beside him once again, propping her sock-clad feet on the coffee table beside his. "I started at Gallimore, Smith & Tomberlin right out of college, and caught the eye of Shawn Gallimore."

Will turned toward her, the hard muscles of his knee nudging hers. "I'm guessing he was one of the partners?"

"Right." Samantha took a long draft of cola, letting the icy liquid slide down her throat. "At first I was just his protégée. He took a…paternal interest in me. And I appreciated all the mentoring, because say what you will about the guy personally, he's an advertising genius."

Will took a small sip. He let the bottle rest on his thigh. "So what changed?"

Samantha let her head fall back against the sofa cushions. She stared at the ceiling above her, marveling at how far away it all seemed. She recounted, "Shawn went through his fourth divorce. He needed a shoulder to cry on, away from the office, and like a fool, I felt sorry for him. I know what it's like to feel…abandoned. The next thing I know, we're having an affair," she confided with a sigh. "Someone saw us one night at a hotel bar, and suddenly everyone in the office knew. Just like that—" Samantha snapped her fingers "—all the hard work I'd put in ceased to matter. I was branded the kind of woman who sleeps her way to the top, while Shawn—well, let's just say I think he got more than one high-five from some of his male colleagues when no one was looking. Anyway, under the circumstances, Shawn thought it would be bad for business for us to continue our affair. I agreed. So we split up, and I transferred to another department, where I would no longer be reporting directly to him. And I hoped that would be the end of it."

"But it wasn't."

"No. The stories about us continued."

"Is Tippi Gallimore wife number four?"

"Five." Samantha rubbed at the pressure points around her eyes, where tension was building. "She married Shawn about four months after he and I called it quits. Which would have been fine except she found out that Shawn and I'd had a thing for a while, and told him he had to fire me."

Will frowned. "That's against the law."

"I know."

He paused, studying her. "You don't want to sue?"

She looked at him. "No."

"Why not?"

Samantha pushed away the dark cloud of regret. "So many reasons. The primary one being that I don't want to waste any more of my life on what was a very big mistake. I just want to move on. The problem is Tippi Gallimore is determined to oust me from the New York City advertising world. So I think, but cannot prove, she has started a whispering campaign about me to make sure no one will want to hire me."

Will set his empty bottle down with a thud and took her hand in his. "All the more reason you should sue the pants off of her," he said firmly.

"You're probably right," Samantha admitted.

"But you're not going to do it."

"Nope." She took another drink, wiping the corners of her lips with the back of her hand.

"You think there's a chance Blount & Levine will hire you?"

"Let's just say they won't *not* hire me because Tippi Gallimore thinks I am bad news."

Will seemed to understand there would be a certain poetic

justice in her getting a job with her old firm's top competitor. "So when will you know if you have a job?" he asked.

That was the good part—she wouldn't have to wait long. "Sometime in the next few days. If I get it, I'll have to start Monday."

Will seemed to have mixed feelings about that, as—surprisingly—did she.

He stood, took her hand and drew her to her feet. "In the meantime, we have tonight."

She noticed he was in no hurry to let her go. "We're not flying back to Laramie tonight?"

He shook his head. "We'll go tomorrow morning. So what do you want to do now? Are you up to showing this Texas pilot a good time?"

Noticing the merriment in his blue eyes, she echoed dryly, "A good time?"

"As opposed to a bad time," he qualified quickly. "Although that could be interesting, too."

Samantha smothered a laugh. "You paying?" she taunted. Because between the clothes she'd purchased in Laramie and her ongoing expenses here, her bank account was dwindling precariously.

"You bet," he said.

First the interview with Blount & Levine. Now this. An evening with Will McCabe, not connected to all the wedding stuff back in Laramie. Life was suddenly looking up. Samantha savored the warmth of their entwined hands, aware she hadn't felt so happy in a long time. "Then you're on."

# Chapter Seven

"Not exactly what you were envisioning, hmm?" Samantha asked, leading the way onto the rooftop of her building.

Will looked at the twinkling lights that extended as far as the eye could see. The panoramic view of the city at night was breathtaking. Made more so by the company he was keeping.

Not that he should be thinking this way, he reminded himself sternly. He wasn't here to get it on with Samantha. He was here to help her in any way she needed, before taking her back to Laramie, where she belonged.

Aware that she was waiting for him to state his opinion, he took another look at the shadowy silhouettes of buildings and the busy streets. The full moon and stars above only added to the romantic allure of the spring evening.

Stuffing his hands in the pockets of his jeans, he swung back around to face her. "It's better than I imagined," he told her, pausing to let her see he meant every word. "You come up here often?"

She took a step closer, her dark eyes seeming to hold more secrets than ever before. She lifted her shoulders in a shrug before continuing the process of setting up their spontaneous picnic. "I hang out up here whenever weather permits."

Will admired the graceful way she moved across the rooftop.

"I especially like it at night when you can see the city lights," Samantha confided.

He helped her carry the wrought-iron café-style table to a spot with a better vantage point, then went back for the matching chairs. Although he had spent most of his childhood in Dallas, he'd never been a city guy. Too many people. Too much noise, traffic, confusion. Yet up here was like being in an oasis he had not expected to encounter, but could not turn away from. "I can see why."

He watched, unsure how to help, as she spread a tablecloth across the small table, then fetched the take-out sacks. She glanced at him curiously, no clue to what else she was thinking or feeling evident. "Sorry you don't live here?" she asked casually.

*Sorry I don't live near you,* Will thought in return, then wondered where that notion had come from. It wasn't like him to get attached to a woman this quickly. Even one as indisputably beautiful as Samantha Holmes. And she was plain gorgeous tonight.

The warm, humid air brought a flush to her skin, and made the loose sexy waves of her dark-cherry hair even wilder. Although he'd admired the interview suit she'd had on earlier, he much preferred her current outfit of low-slung jeans, running shoes and a stretchy long-sleeved T-shirt that bared her navel every time she moved. As much as Will had tried not to notice, it was an indisputable fact—she had a very sexy navel. He needed to stop looking at it, stop wondering if her abdomen was as silky and taut to the touch as it appeared. He had to stop thinking about kissing her again. Kissing her there.

Oblivious to his indecent thoughts, she handed him the matches and he lit the hurricane candle. Grateful for some way to help, he opened up the paper sacks of Chinese takeout and removed the white cardboard cartons. He settled opposite her in one of the wrought-iron chairs, stretching his long legs out in front of him. "So is the view the reason you chose an apartment in this building?" he asked, lifting a spring roll to his mouth.

She shook her head and went after the crab wontons. "It was the cheapest place I could find, close to a subway stop, that still left me money in the budget for the clothes I desperately needed for work."

"You looked spectacular in the business suit you had on today."

She riffled through the boxes, handing him the kung pao chicken, taking the sweet-and-sour pork for herself. "Everyone looks good in Armani."

He paused, chopsticks halfway to his lips. "Why do you do that?"

She took a bite and swallowed. "Deflect a compliment?"

"Yes."

She cast her eyes toward the exquisite skyline. "It's the truth."

"That you looked mighty fine today, yes, it is." But then, he added silently to himself, she always looked mighty fine. It didn't matter what she wore or what she was doing, she looked beautiful. More so every day.

Samantha kicked back in her chair, tilted her head, as if holding it that way would give her a greater understanding of what was going on inside of him. Silky hair fell across her shoulders, onto her breast. Slowly, the corners of her lips turned upward. "Will McCabe," she chided softly. "Are you trying to seduce me?"

*I wish.* Unfortunately, the gallantry deeply ingrained in all McCabe men had him holding back. Samantha still had a lot to work out. Getting involved with him at this juncture—well, it probably wouldn't help the confusion she was obviously struggling with. It might even make things worse for her.

Wishing he didn't want to pull her out of that chair and onto his lap quite so badly, Will drawled, "Do you want me to seduce you?"

She chuckled. "Do you always answer a question with a question?"

He grinned. "Do you?"

Her smile widened as the flirtatious mood between them deepened. She went back to eating a crispy spring roll.

Feeling the pressure building at the front of his jeans, Will decided to dial it back a notch, for both their sakes. Searching for a pedestrian subject, he exchanged cartons with her, finally asked, "Do you like living in the city?"

She nodded. Her expression sobering, she helped herself to some of the kung pao chicken. "You seem surprised," she noted.

No shock there, Will thought. Anyone from the Lone Star State would entertain the same question. "After having grown up in Texas, I'd think you would miss the wide-open spaces."

A furrow formed along the bridge of her nose. "That's why we have Central Park."

He wasn't buying her perplexed act for a minute. "You know what I mean."

Yes, she did. It didn't mean she would answer him, he noted.

After a few more bites, she waved her hand in front of her, as if that would dispel the spicy heat. She opened her bottle of iced mango tea, took a long cooling sip and lightly pounded her chest.

"Too spicy?"

"Understatement," she responded between gasps, taking another long gulp of tea. Wiping tears from her eyes, she asked in a low, throaty voice that conjured up forbidden images of damp sheets and hot bodies, "What about you?" She put down her chopsticks and looked him in the eye. "I presume you went all over the world during your years in the navy."

"Yep. I did." And nothing he had seen or experienced in all that time held a candle to the thrill going through him now.

Appearing to enjoy being with him as much as he liked

spending time with her, she lifted the icy-cold bottle to her cheek, pressed it there, letting the chill transmit to her skin.

"What took you back to Texas?" she prodded.

Glad the interest wasn't one-sided, he quipped, "Ah, the usual suspects."

Her dark eyes lit up. "Such as?"

Will spoke with the same gravity with which he would have referred to the Holy Grail. "Family. Barbecue. Tex-Mex."

"Ah." Recovered, she pushed back in her chair and concentrated on her beverage. "So it's true—" she lifted her bottle in a mock toast "—the way to a man's heart is through his stomach."

Will couldn't deny there was something to that. Good food, good company, an incredibly sexy woman all went a long way toward making a memorable evening.

He let his glance linger on her softly parted lips. "If that's the case, you've outdone yourself," he complimented her warmly. "This takeout is fantastic."

"Thanks." She tossed him a plastic-wrapped fortune cookie. "But you paid for it."

"You dialed."

He broke open his cookie.

So did she. "What does yours say?" she asked.

"'Adventure lies ahead.' And yours?"

Samantha made a face. Clearly, Will thought, she was not a believer in Chinese wisdom.

She read the print on the small white slip of paper. "'Good fortune is coming your way.'"

He made no effort to hide his disappointment. "A little generic." He'd been hoping her fortune would say something about hot romance with the perfect guy, or something to that effect.

"You think?" Samantha exhaled, her expression turning more wistful than ever.

Will noticed she didn't throw her fortune away, however. Rather, she slipped it into the pocket of her jeans.

Figuring at the very least he'd have a memento of the evening, he did the same with his. Then added, "Never hurts to have a positive outlook on life."

Samantha thought about that for a second. "I guess you're right."

"Could you ever see yourself living in Texas again?"

She tensed, on guard once more. "Are you asking for Howard?"

Will shook his head slowly, surprised by the realization. "Myself," he admitted.

Uncertainty flickered in her eyes. "Why?" she whispered.

That, at least, was easy. "Because—" Will reached over and touched her hand "—I'd like to continue seeing you."

SURPRISED—AND YET NOT—Samantha stood and began cleaning up. Her legs trembled and butterflies took over her middle. This was what she secretly wanted, as well as what she guarded against. An entanglement with a man who had the power to change her carefully constructed life.

Looking disappointed by her careful nonreaction, Will pitched in to help. "I gather that's a no?" he said in that husky voice of his.

Alarmed that she had let her inherent cynicism take a back seat to the desire building steadily inside her, Samantha came up with the first excuse she could locate. "You're not old enough for me," she fibbed, acting as if her mind weren't on all the steamy options that were never going to be explored between the two of them.

He looked at her as if he had never heard that one before. And wouldn't mind disabusing her of the notion. "I'm thirty-six," he said dryly.

Determined not to let him see how much his pursuit was affecting her, Samantha lifted an insouciant brow. "And I'm thirty."

He moved the table and chairs back where they'd found them. He straightened, his eyes holding hers. "The age difference doesn't sound insurmountable to me."

Samantha ignored the shimmer of sexual attraction between them. She let her eyes rove over his tall, solidly built frame and powerful shoulders. "I like much older men," she continued to fib.

He wasn't buying it. He came closer. She could feel his body heat and breathed in the enticing fragrance of his cologne.

"Daddy complex, hmm?" He spoke above the sound of a car horn on the street below.

Telling herself she was much too smart to be drawn into a convenient affair with this very sexy man, she gathered up the trash and led the way to the door. "Something like that."

He followed her down the stairs, past her apartment, to the garbage receptacles in the alley. "I don't think that's it."

Samantha dropped the sacks in the bin, then turned and glowered at Will as she struggled to get a handle on her soaring emotions. "So now you're an expert on psychology," she noted, having discovered firsthand what it would be like to be the recipient of his interest.

He held the door for her. "Just on you."

Samantha led the way up the stairs. Being back in New York City gave her confidence, made her feel more in control of the situation. "And what have you concluded?" She paused just outside her door.

He rubbed his jaw in a thoughtful manner. His gaze took her in, head to toe. "That you avoid men closer to your own age because we're dangerous."

Not everyone, she thought, ushering him back inside. Just Will McCabe. Going straight to the sink, she poured soap on her hands and lathered up her palms.

Will angled in beside her, washing his own hands. "Dangerous how?" she asked, her heart kicking against her ribs.

Together, they rinsed their hands under the tap.

Will waited until they had shared a towel before he cupped her shoulders gently and replied, "Dangerous in that when we younger guys hold you and kiss you, we do it like we mean it."

Samantha felt he certainly would. Not about to let him know that, she choked out, "That's not true."

Will gave her a sexy half smile. Sliding his hands down her arms, he caught her wrists in his grasp and moved them around the small of her back so she was arched against him. "It is for me."

And just that suddenly, his lips found hers. This kiss was every bit as magical as before and her body jolted from the pure pleasure of it. She heard herself make a sound that was part whimper, part sigh. She opened her mouth to the pressure of his, aware she hadn't made out like this since she didn't know when. Despite her earlier determination to remain friendly but emotionally aloof, Samantha felt her defenses begin to crumble. The bantering they'd exchanged, the confidences, were nothing compared to the heat and intimacy of this moment in time. Nothing compared to how much more she wanted from him.

With one warm palm still pressed against her waist, holding her close, Will slipped the other beneath the hem of her T-shirt to caress her abdomen and ribs, before moving to her breasts. Her skin sizzled. Her nipples budded against the flat of his open hand. Sensation layered upon sensation. And still they kissed and kissed and kissed. To the point that she knew with much more of this there'd be no turning back. No way would she be able to prevent getting emotionally involved.

"Will..." she murmured helplessly against his mouth. Wanting. Needing. Wishing. Even as she feared the ramifications that such an attachment might bring...

He threaded both hands through her hair and gazed at her in a way that let her know he wanted her desperately, too. "Just kiss me, Samantha," he whispered, with heat in his eyes, tenderness in his touch.

And kiss him she did, surrendering to his will until she was so dizzy she could barely stand, until desire unfurled like a ribbon inside her and her thighs were liquid and weak. Until she was clinging to him, trembling.

His lips moved from her mouth to the slope of her neck. "I want you," he said, kissing her collarbone, her chin, the tender spot behind her ear.

The surprising thing was she wanted him, too. More than she had ever expected.

"And yet I'm thinking," he continued, with the legendary McCabe gallantly, "that maybe I should leave before things get out of hand and you resent the hell out of me in the morning."

Samantha took a deep breath, feeling simultaneously grateful for his concern and disappointed it wasn't going to happen tonight.

She also knew he was right. If he made love to her now, on a whim, she would likely feel taken advantage of come morning.

She flattened her hands across his chest and pushed backward. She would go the honorable route, too, despite her wish to throw caution to the wind, for once, and just follow her heart.

She released a wistful little sigh. "I'm not going to resent you in the morning because nothing else is going to happen tonight."

WILL KNEW SAMANTHA WAS only doing the sensible thing—taking the guarded approach to whatever was developing between them.

Nevertheless, he couldn't help but feel disappointed that she hadn't said to heck with waiting, and jumped his bones then and there. Rolling around in the sheets, their naked bodies pressed together, would have been a really nice way to end the evening. Not to mention waking up wrapped in each other's arms.

"Just because we're adults and there's an attraction between us," Samantha explained practically, taking out a stack of linens and two pillows from the drawers in the steamer chest that served as her coffee table, "does not mean we have to act on it."

At least one of them was now being completely rational. Noting how sexy she looked with her hair tousled, her cheeks pink, her lips damp and swollen from his kisses, Will followed her around the small apartment, wishing all the while he could run his hands through the silky waves of her hair once again. He stood behind her, thumbs in his belt loops, trying not to lust after the delectable curves of her backside. "True enough."

"We already slept in a single bed without giving in to temptation," Samantha reminded him.

She thrust the linens at him, then bent to remove the seat cushions and pull out the bed that had been tucked away. "This sofa bed is a queen..." She chatted on endlessly, leaving him to contemplate what a lovely body she had, and just how far he was from paying homage to such perfection. "And we'll have the benefit of a rolled up blanket between us."

Which would do nothing, Will knew, to quell his raging fantasies about making Samantha his.

Nevertheless, he knew this was a test he had to pass if he wanted to get closer to her—and he did. He had to prove to her that he wouldn't walk out on her and wouldn't cross any boundaries she established. Even if it was only a blanket rolled up in the middle of a sofa bed.

"You're right," he said cheerfully, deciding his fate for the evening could have been worse. She could have kicked him out, told him she wasn't going back to Texas and never wanted to see him again.

Visibly relieved he was taking her rules so well, Samantha slipped into the bathroom to get ready for bed, and then fell asleep almost the moment her head hit the pillow.

Will stared at the ceiling, his arms folded behind his head, listening to the soft sound of her breathing, drinking in the familiar scent of her hair and skin.

He was nearly asleep himself when he heard her swift intake of breath, felt her start to shudder, saw the tears sliding down her face. She curled into herself, crying harder now.

Unable to lie there beside her and do nothing, he removed the barrier between them, pulled her close and held her against him until the shuddering stopped, her tears subsided and she was peaceful once again.

SAMANTHA WOKE to the sound of the phone ringing, and the sturdy warmth of Will's body pressed up against hers. The blanket that had been supposed to serve as protection lay across their feet.

When the phone continued ringing, she reached for it, pulling the receiver to her ear. "Hello."

A crisp voice answered.

Realizing this was business, she struggled to a sitting position, listening intently to everything being said. "Absolutely. Yes. Monday at nine. I'll see you then."

Still stunned, she set the receiver back on its base and turned to see Will propped up on one elbow watching her. Clad only in a pair of low-slung pajama pants, his hair delectably rumpled and his face dark with beard, he looked incredibly sexy. Passing on the chance to make wild, reckless love with him suddenly seemed more foolish than wise.

"Who was it?" His voice rumbled from deep inside his chest.

Samantha instructed her heart to slow down. If she and Will were meant to connect that way, there was still time. "That was the human resources director at Blount & Levine. I got the job," she murmured, hardly able to believe her good fortune. "I start Monday."

An indefinable emotion flickered in his blue eyes, then was gone.

"Congratulations." He smiled warmly.

She wondered if he would be glad to see her vanish from his life at the end of the week—or as sad as she knew she was going to be.

"I can't believe it." Still feeling a little groggy, and warm all over, Samantha raked her hands through her hair, doing her best to restore order to the tousled mess. "After months of looking, finally I have a job." She sat up, bringing her knees to her chest, and wreathed her arms around them.

Relief flowed through her. No more worrying about how to scrape up the money to pay rent. Or if she would ever be hired in New York City again. No more eating peanut butter sandwiches for days on end, and apples bought in bulk. No more wondering if it had been all that smart, investing in great work clothes instead of mutual funds.

Joy bubbled up inside her, right next to a very fine sense of accomplishment. "This is a big deal, Will."

"I can see that," he said with an amused grin.

"Blount & Levine is a top five firm."

He reached over and squeezed her knee, genuinely happy for her. "They'll be lucky to have you."

Unable to stay still a moment longer, Samantha hopped out of bed. "And the salary is nothing to sneeze at, either." She went into the bathroom and grabbed her toothbrush. Will followed slowly, looking more delectably handsome than ever.

"I'll be making ten percent more—to start—than I was at Gallimore, Smith & Tomberlin when I left."

He watched her layer paste onto the brush, and teased, "The only question is are you going to spend it on more clothes or a better address?"

Samantha stopped brushing long enough to make a face at him. She appreciated his sense of humor as much as his praise. She rinsed and spat. "Hey, I know my quarters could be larger and more luxurious, but for New York City, this place isn't half-bad." She blotted her mouth with a towel.

He stepped up beside her at the sink and reached for his toiletries kit. "I'll take your word on it."

They smiled. He seemed happy that she was happy. It was a good feeling to share her success with someone, Samantha thought, opening the blinds to let the sunshine in. It had been even better to wake up wrapped in Will's arms. Speaking of which… Samantha paused next to the sofa bed, looked at the rumpled blanket that should have still been rolled up in the center of the mattress. "How did that get to the bottom?" she asked.

Will emerged from the bathroom, drying his mouth with the same navy blue hand towel she'd used. "I threw it there."

Samantha blinked. "Why?"

He came closer. "You were crying in your sleep again," he informed her gently, cupping her chin in his hand. "It broke my heart to see you hurting that way, even if you weren't awake."

She had the feeling he wanted to take her in his arms and kiss her again. She didn't want that to happen when she was feeling so vulnerable, didn't want to worry that even a part of the reason for his involvement was because he felt sympathy for her.

She rubbed her hands over her bare arms, chasing away the sudden chill. "It's got to be the wedding, seeing Howard again."

Will studied her, taking in her pink camisole sleep top and mismatched pajama bottoms, before returning his gaze to her face.

"Sure that's all it is?" he asked.

Samantha swallowed, refusing to think about the guilt and pain that had haunted her for years now. "It has to be," she said.

WILL FELT COMFORTABLE going to his stepmother for advice and guidance. Kate was a great listener. She didn't ask the kind of questions that would keep him from confiding in her. She always knew what to do. Always had time to talk to him, even when she was at the hospital, getting ready to leave for a speaking gig in San Antonio.

"It could be post-traumatic stress syndrome," Kate theorized, after Will had filled her in on Samantha's nocturnal weeping. "A repressed memory. Or even something Samantha recalls very well but isn't willing to share with you."

Will lounged against the wall. "How do I know the difference?"

"You wait for her to trust you enough to tell you."

Frustration turned down the corners of his mouth. "That could take months."

"Yes. It could." Kate paused. "How did Samantha and Howard become orphaned?"

"I don't know that, either."

"But both of them grew up in Texas, right?"

"Right. Beaumont."

Kate studied him with a mother's knowing eyes. "You're beginning to care about Samantha, aren't you?"

More than that, Will thought. Crazy as it sounded, he could see himself in love with her. For all the good it was going to do him, given her reluctance to put her heart on the line.

He shrugged and slid his hands in the back pockets of his jeans, aware that if he wasn't careful he would end up on the losing end of the stick, too. "She just took another job in New York City. She starts Monday."

"What does that have to do with your feelings?" Kate asked, not the least dissuaded.

Will told himself he could handle a short-term fling, if that was all Samantha could commit to. Especially if doing so would allow him to help her get to a place where she stopped reliving the traumas from her early life. Not about to admit that, however, he stated casually, "No point in starting something that only has to end."

Kate wasn't fooled by his cavalier attitude. But then, Will noted, she never had been.

"Ever heard of a long-distance romance?"

Will grimaced. "Tried it once, remember? It didn't work for me."

Kate went back to packing up papers. "Maybe you just married the wrong woman."

Another beat of silence fell between them. "Have you tried talking to Howard about what could be bothering his sister?" she finally murmured.

Will shook his head.

"Why not?"

This was harder to explain. "It's not the kind of thing a guy asks another guy. Besides, then I'd have to tell him how I know what she does in her sleep." Howard knew Samantha was sleeping in Will's cramped personal quarters at the airstrip. He didn't know the two of them had shared a bed. Will wanted to keep it that way. Not because he was ashamed, but because he knew how it looked. And it hadn't been that way at all. Kate understood that. Sort of. Howard probably wouldn't. Nor would Will if he were in Howard's place.

Kate closed her briefcase and came around to perch on the side of her desk. "I'd like to talk to you about that myself. You have to get her out of your quarters at the airstrip and into more suitable lodgings."

Will straightened. "She has a standing invitation from both Molly and Howard. I was hoping my lack of chivalry would force her to accept their offer, if only for comfort's sake. Unfortunately, she refused."

"No surprise there." Kate regarded him gently. "You can't manipulate someone into doing what you want, and expect to get positive results. Take Howard, for instance. He has bullied Samantha into participating in his wedding to Molly, but Samantha's heart isn't in it and she's only going to resent him more in the end."

Which was maybe why he should never have agreed to lobby on Howard's behalf and "soften" Samantha up, Will thought. But it was too late now. Like it or not, he was involved. And he didn't want to see her continue to hurt.

"It's always better to deal directly with people than try to maneuver them surreptitiously," Kate continued.

Will gave her a wry grin, surrendering to her greater wisdom and vast experience in dealing with people. "Now you tell me," he joked, looking her straight in the eye.

His stepmom pushed away from her desk, plucked her purse out of a desk drawer and rummaged through it. "Look, the first thing we have to do is get Samantha some personal space and much needed privacy for the duration of the week."

Will wasn't sure he liked the sound of that. He liked being able to keep an eye on her and be there in case she needed him.

"Good luck," he told his stepmother. "All the local hotels are filled with people attending the state agricultural extension courses."

Car keys in hand, Kate replied. "I think I can manage it. Just tell me where I can find her."

IN AN EFFORT TO GIVE Samantha the space Kate felt she needed, Will did not go back to his office at the airstrip—where Samantha was working on the advertising campaign. Instead, he went over to his parents' house on Spring Street, fixed himself some lunch and then holed up in his father's study. Using the information on his PDA, he printed out the week's flight schedule for his company, then picked up the phone and began calling the pilots who worked for him. An hour later, he had arranged to be off until the following Monday, and began doing some research of his own.

It took a while, but eventually he found what he needed in the *Beaumont Daily Register* archives online. The headline of the article alone was enough to sucker punch him in the gut: Boating Accident Claims Parents, Two Children Survive.

Will had just started to read the devastating account when the front door opened. Footsteps sounded in the foyer, then Samantha stood framed in the doorway, hauling the additional suitcase of clothing and laptop computer she had brought back with her from New York. "What are you doing here?" she demanded, looking none too pleased to find the house occupied.

Figuring his fact-finding would have to wait until later, Will bookmarked the page and quickly got the article off the screen. "Working." He leaned back in the desk chair and clasped his hands behind his head. "What are you doing here?"

"I talked to your stepmother. Kate offered me a house-sitting gig for the rest of the week. She said she was going to a psych conference, your dad is in California on business and neither of them will be back until Sunday afternoon. I'm supposed to be here alone."

"Well, there's a problem with that." Will grimaced, wishing he had asked Kate her plans before she'd put them into action. "I just offered my quarters to the pilot taking my flights for the rest of the week."

Samantha set her belongings down with a clatter. "He can't sleep in his own place?"

"The guy who is subbing for me lives in Wichita Falls. He wasn't expecting to have to work this week, and there are no hotel rooms available."

"So you were kicking me out of the airstrip?"

"No. I was going to ask my parents if it was okay, and offer you lodgings here."

"With you."

Actually, Will had been planning to bunk with one of his four married brothers—all of whom lived in the area—until he had read the archived news report. Now there was no way in hell he was going to leave her alone, to struggle against what had to be debilitating memories. Any more than he would have ever left a buddy behind in battle. He didn't care how it looked.

"This place is plenty big enough for the two of us," Will stated lazily, doing his best to hide the compassion welling up inside him. The rambling Victorian had housed Kate and Sam and their six kids comfortably. "It has seven bedrooms and four and a half baths. I'll take my old room. You can have my sister's old bedroom. We'll never even have to see each other if we don't want to."

"Did your stepmother know this was going to be the case?"

"No. And I'm sure she won't approve. Kate wanted me away from you."

"Smart woman." Samantha continued to scowl at Will.

"You can always go to Molly's place."

"Thanks but no thanks. But as long as you *are* here, make yourself useful and carry my stuff upstairs to the room where I'm going to be staying," she continued. "Then I've got to change clothes." She sighed loudly and gave him a vaguely accusing look. "I have to go over to the Nedermeyers and take care of their pets."

Will wondered if she had heard the stories. "You don't seem as enthusiastic about that as before," he noted, rising to do her bidding.

Samantha rolled her eyes. "That's because I didn't know the backyard pets they'd mentioned and 'the kids' were one and the same—until I got over there at noon to go over their instructions." She whirled around, then shot him a glare over her shoulder. "You could have told me, you know."

"I figured you knew and were just being…adventurous."

She stopped so suddenly he ran into her back, knocking them both off-kilter. "Please."

He steadied her slender frame with a light touch, regretting when she bolted on up the front staircase, looking not the least bit affected by their fleeting contact. "And then there's the fact you haven't really seemed to want my advice," he added, only to have her round on him. "Look, I'll help you take care of them," he offered, even though cleaning out pens wasn't really his thing.

She waved her hand and kept going. "I've got it covered." Samantha paused in the doorway of an impossibly frilly pink-and-white room, complete with canopy bed, white furniture and floral wallpaper. "This where I'm staying?"

"Yep. You can use the bathroom across the hall. I'll use the one at the other end of the house, toward my bedroom. Towels and shampoo and everything should be in there."

"Thanks."

He leaned against the doorjamb, watching her walk around Laurel's old bedroom, taking it all in. He wondered how the frilly excess compared with the places she had bunked in foster care. "You going to the bachelorette party for Molly this evening?"

Samantha exhaled loudly. "I had hoped to get out of it, but since I missed the couples shower yesterday, I feel I have to go." She looked to be dreading it more than she would ever say. "What about you?" Her voice sounded husky. She met his eyes. "Going to the bachelor party?"

Will nodded, aware once again that Samantha seemed to have the weight of the world on her shoulders. He knew how that felt.

He'd felt lost and alone when his mom died and his dad had been unreachable in his grief. The resulting stress had driven he and his brothers apart.

Luckily for them, Kate had come into their lives. She'd used her skills as a grief counselor to help them deal with the loss and become a family again. She'd married his dad, and given them a little sister.

Will knew he was lucky. His life had returned to normal within a couple of years. He didn't think Samantha's ever had. But that could change. All he had to do was figure out how to help.

# *Chapter Eight*

Samantha fought back tears as she closed the door behind her and began to change into jeans, T-shirt and sneakers. She didn't know why she suddenly felt so emotional. Except maybe because going from one unknown environment to another, suitcase in hand, reminded her of all the different places she had lived as a kid. Never knowing how long she would be there, if the people would be kind or cold. Only knowing she was alone. And that it was her own fault, more than anyone's.

Not that she could afford to be stressing out over this, with the evening ahead. Getting through the bachelorette party, pretending yet again that nothing was wrong, was going to be even more of a challenge than battling painful memories. Samantha couldn't believe Howard was letting Molly do this to her—except that he had never taken pains to consider her feelings in the past.

The only good part of her day had been meeting Kate McCabe. Will's stepmother was wonderful and warmly intuitive beneath her practical exterior.

"Life has thrown me a few curve balls, too," Kate had told her, handing her a business card with all her numbers scrawled on the back. "Having married a McCabe and helped rear five others, I know how difficult the McCabe men can be. So if you ever find yourself at wit's end, or want to talk, or even need me to get Will to back off and stop making your life so darn difficult, you just call. I'll be happy to help."

It was only later, when Kate had left, that Samantha turned the card over and saw that Kate was affiliated with the local hospital as a therapist who specialized in grief counseling.

Which made Samantha wonder just how much the woman knew about her.

Determined, however, to get through the rest of this day as stalwartly as she had everything else undesirable in her life, Samantha headed out, leaving the McCabes' cozy abode. Appreciating the tree-lined streets and beautifully maintained turn-of-the-century Victorians, she walked the block and a half to the Nedermeyers'. When she went around back, through the fence, she gasped at what she saw.

"LOOKS LIKE YOU'VE GOT your work cut out for you," a low voice said from somewhere behind her.

Samantha whirled and saw Will lounging on a wooden bench beneath a tree. He had one arm resting along the back, his legs stretched out and crossed at the ankles. He, too, was dressed casually. Unlike her, he seemed ready to have a little fun.

"How did you get here before I did?" Samantha asked, not sure whether to be relieved or perturbed.

The truth was, she was a little uneasy at the prospect of taking care of the forty-pound animals. Hansel and Gretel looked cute as could be, with their handsome button eyes and antennae ears, but she had been warned the duo could be mischievous, especially with strangers.

Fortunately, they were show goats, not dairy goats. She didn't know what she would do if she had to milk them, too!

At the moment, though, they just looked sort of sad and…anxious.

Will joined her beside the pen. Her irritated tone had

brought a provoking grin to his face. He locked eyes with her for a long moment, then looked pointedly down at the pets. "I left the house before you did and cut through a couple of yards."

"Well, you can go home the same way," Samantha retorted, shooing him away.

It was easy to tell Hansel and Gretel apart—Hansel had whiskers under his chin. They were actually quite handsome with their short, stocky bodies, silver-gray fur, black stockings and dark faces.

"I have no intention of providing your entertainment for the day," Samantha scolded Will.

Respect glimmered in his blue eyes even as Will pinched his nose. "Nothing funny about that mess in there," he drawled. Or the smell.

Samantha looked back at the piles of muck strewn across the concrete floor of the pen. "What happened?" she asked, genuinely concerned. "Do you think we should call the vet?" The pets had been fine earlier, when she'd been receiving instructions on how to care for them.

Looking more relaxed than ever, Will shook his head wryly. "Upset stomachs due to stress. Happens every time the Nedermeyers leave."

Which explained, Samantha thought, the reluctant, slightly apprehensive looks on the couple's faces as she'd left the get-to-meet-the-kids session.

"Everyone here knows about it," Will continued, chuckling.

"Looking back on what was said, I think they assumed I did, too," Samantha mused out loud, realizing she was responsible for getting herself into this situation.

"But they didn't come right out and say it," Will concluded.

Samantha shrugged, a self-conscious flush flooding her face. "They alluded to the difficulties of caring for such emotionally sensitive pets. Which, I have to tell you, I dismissed out of hand as the usual overprotective pet owner thing."

Will nodded.

She cleared her throat. "Nevertheless, after making the introductions and realizing I hadn't understood the 'kids' were actually goats, they gave me several opportunities to gracefully bow out. But I thought that was just because they considered me a city slicker and therefore somehow incompetent at anything the least bit, uh, rural."

He understood how that might have rankled her. "And you were determined to prove yourself as capable as the next Texan," he teased.

Once again amazed at his ability to see right through her, Samantha made a face at him. "I *am* as capable as the next Texan," she declared heatedly.

He flashed a wicked grin that dared her to prove it.

Rather than get enmeshed in a conversation that would soon have her kissing him again, she went back to discussing how she had landed in such a predicament. "Anyway, the initial misunderstanding aside, I figured caring for goats in a backyard pen couldn't be much different than caring for a dog or a cat—both of which I did many a time, while I was working my way through college."

Looking as if he wasn't sure he agreed with that, Will inclined his head toward the pen where Hansel and Gretel sat, watching the two humans patiently. "Ever have this problem then?" he asked.

"Yes, unfortunately," Samantha admitted, remembering one lonely, stressed out bulldog that had had her taking him outside every thirty minutes during one very long night. "But not to this extent." She sighed, looking at the mess she was going to have clean up. Glad to see that Hansel and Gretel's stomachs had apparently settled, she shook her head. " No wonder the Nedermeyers have a heck of a time finding anyone to goat-sit."

Will moved closer. "I'm still surprised they asked you."

Aware she had never been this distracted by a man before, and that Will seemed equally enamored of her, Samantha admitted with a rueful chuckle, "They didn't. I volunteered. They were talking to someone at the party about the difficulty of finding anyone to care for their pets when Molly introduced me. I heard about the money they were offering and figured…why not?"

"Especially since you were short on cash right then," Will guessed.

She nodded. "They were really reluctant to accept my offer of assistance, since I was just in town for Molly and Howard's wedding. But I assured them I had years of experience pet- and house-sitting and would love to do it, particularly since it was only for a couple of days." Samantha shook her head as she thought about what she had gotten herself into.

He listened patiently as she recounted the events that had led to the current debacle.

"Now, of course, I see their dilemma," Samantha continued, pausing to pet Hansel and Gretel through the fence. "Why they had to accept my help unless they wanted to ask their friends and neighbors again, which they felt they had done far too often in the past."

Will came over to pet the animals, too. "It's true the Nedermeyers' options were limited, since you can't board a goat at a kennel like you do a cat or dog."

So here she was. Facing two anxious animals and one heck of a mess.

Will walked over to the row of sturdy vinyl boots sitting beside the pen, and tossed her some smaller ones. "I suggest we put on Wellingtons before we start."

She watched him slip the large boots over his running shoes, then did the same.

She knew he wanted to get her in the sack. But this was too much to ask of any man, no matter how hot his pursuit.

She studied him bluntly. "You're really going to help?"

He shrugged, as if it was no big deal. "Consider it my good deed for the day."

He might as well have been wearing a halo. "You're making it hard for me to…"

"Think poorly of me?" he guessed, when she didn't finish.

She'd been going to say "resist you," but figured she liked his answer better, since it was less revealing. "That's the general idea," she quipped.

Wishing she could hold her nose, Samantha donned disposable latex work gloves from the dispenser mounted just outside the fence, and stepped into the pen where Hansel and Gretel resided. A cement floor, covered with hay, fronted a three-sided gingerbread goat "cottage" painted with their names. A six-foot chain-link fence surrounded the structure. There were toys and water and food dishes. Most dogs didn't have it this good.

Unfortunately, the goats—having abruptly decided they trusted Samantha and Will to care for them, after all—wanted to play with the end of the rakes, which made it impossible to get anything done in regard to cleanup. Samantha turned around to look at the backyard. The white picket fence was waist high and totally enclosed the lawn. Making an executive decision, she opened the gate. "You all go out in the yard and play while we do this."

Will gave her a warning look.

"It will be fine," Samantha said.

"If you say so."

Hansel sniffed the grass, while Gretel lay down in the shade. "I do."

"Get anything done on the ad campaign today?" Will asked.

Nodding, Samantha raked, while he filled a bucket with water from the garden hose, and disinfectant soap.

"I found three golf resorts willing to go in on a package deal," she related as Will scrubbed the concrete with a long-handled brush and rinsed it clean with the hose. "One in Georgia, two in South Carolina. You can play on those courses year-round, so it looks like a good deal. And two spas are interested. One in Arizona, the other Florida. The discounts we talked about ranged from five to twenty percent on packages. To take it further and nail down the fine print on the proposed deals, you'll have to get the lawyers involved. I've got all the information on my laptop. There are copies of it in your office at the airstrip."

Will glanced at her admiringly. "Fast work."

Samantha disposed of the soiled straw, the way the Nedermeyers had shown her. "Good ideas usually come together quickly."

While she filled the feed and water dishes, Will spread clean straw. "How long will it take to get ads ready for the newspapers?" he asked.

"It can be done in a matter of days once the deals are finalized." Samantha stripped off her gloves, tossed them into the tall metal trash barrel.

"Are you going to be able to handle that, what with your new job back East?"

That, Samantha realized, was her only regret. She wanted a reason to see Will, or at least talk to him regularly, even if she was no longer in Texas.

"Not unless you want to pay Blount & Levine rates for my services. It would be a conflict of interest for me to do it on the side." She squirted soap from the dispenser outside the pen and started washing her hands.

Will put away his cleaning tools and followed suit. For a moment he looked as disappointed as she felt about that. "And that could get you fired."

"Right. But I'll get you set up with someone affordable when I…" As Samantha spoke, she looked behind her and saw an empty yard.

Will followed her glance. "Where are Hansel and Gretel?"

"Oh, no. No." Samantha looked around frantically.

"They must have jumped the fence," Will noted, appearing as tense as Samantha felt.

The two of them rushed around to the front of the Neder-meyer home, looked up and down the street.

"I don't see them," Samantha said, beginning to panic.

"But I see where they've been." Will pointed at a flowerbed that'd been recently trampled and had blossoms bitten off. "We'll just follow the signs of destruction."

"What happens if we can't find them?"

"We'll find them," Will stated grimly. "Goats chomping off flowers do not go unnoticed."

Two streets over, Hansel and Gretel were munching on a bed of bluebonnets next to the front porch of a Craftsman style home. Seeing Samantha and Will, they trotted on. Will touched her arm. "You keep following them at a leisurely rate. I'll go around the other way."

He disappeared between two houses, and Samantha hurried to catch up with the goats. To her dismay, the quicker she went, the faster they traveled. When she slowed down and pre-tended not to care, they went back to snapping leaves off shrubs and blossoms from flowerbeds.

Will peeked around the side of a house, motioned wildly for her to call them. Hoping this plan worked, Samantha knelt on the sidewalk. "Here, Hansel. Here, Gretel…"

They ignored her.

She called louder.

They turned to look at her once again. Will came up behind them and managed to snatch Gretel up under his arm. Hansel ran the other way. Samantha swore and took off after him, leaving Will behind. Twice, she almost caught up with the gray-and-black goat, only to have him escape again. She rounded the corner of another house, determined to catch him this time, only to see Hansel had already found a friend.

The lovestruck former schoolteacher, Oscar Gentry, had the ornery pet eating out of his hand.

"THANKS FOR COMING TO our rescue." Panting, Samantha doubled over, hands on her knees. She struggled to catch her breath.

Will jogged up behind her, Hansel tucked under his arm, football style. "Hey, Mr. Gentry."

"Will." His old teacher settled on the steps of the house his wife still occupied, and started to rub the goat behind the ears. "I'm glad you're both here," he said.

Samantha looked at the beautiful crystal vase of pink roses sitting in front of the screen door. "I'm glad the Nedermeyers' goats didn't eat those flowers. Did you bring them for your wife?"

Mr. Gentry nodded, disconsolate. "For all the good it will do me. I followed your advice, Samantha. I've serenaded her, left her love letters, had her favorite kind of breakfast scone delivered, fresh from the bakery. All to no avail. She still won't even come out on the porch to talk to me."

"Is she home now?"

"No. She's at her Daughters of Texas historical literature meeting. That's how I knew it was safe to bring the flowers. I figured she would see them when she got home…." His voice trailed off in discouragement.

Will summed up the situation and took charge. "Let's get these goats home and then we'll talk."

The three of them took a few shortcuts across lawns. Five minutes later, Hansel and Gretel were back in their pen, set for the night. The trio headed for Sam and Kate McCabe's home. Samantha settled on the veranda with Mr. Gentry, while Will went inside to get cold drinks.

He returned with three cans of cherry cola.

"I'm thinking I need to try a new tack, because courting Yvonne the way I used to just isn't working," Oscar Gentry concluded, bringing both of them up to speed.

"I wouldn't necessarily say that," Samantha mused, propping her chin on her fist. "Has she asked you to stop? Told you to go away? Not to bother with any of it?"

"No."

"Trust me, if she really wanted you to quit she would make that very clear to you. All she would have to do is call the sheriff's department, or serve you with divorce papers or a restraining order. The fact that she hasn't," Samantha continued thoughtfully, "means she is at least willing to let you express your continued devotion to her. But you're right, if what you have done thus far hasn't gotten you the reaction you want, then a revamping of the campaign to win back your wife's affections is in order."

Mr. Gentry stared at the bluebonnets rimming the porch. "I can't write poetry worth a darn. If I could, I'd do that." He tapped a finger on the rim of the can. "So I was thinking, maybe if I put something in the Laramie newspaper…?"

"Like a personal ad?" Samantha asked.

Mr. Gentry shrugged. "It works for people on TV."

"That's an…interesting idea," she replied.

"I'll get a paper and pen." Will disappeared inside the house again.

"The only thing is," Mr. Gentry muttered, " I haven't a clue what to say."

Neither did Samantha. "Does the Laramie newspaper generally run personal ads?" she asked curiously.

"Only on Valentine's Day. Then they do a fun thing, special to that edition. But they always have classified ads."

"So if we put it under the heading 'Wanted…'" Samantha reached over, accepting pen and paper from Will.

"They'd probably print it," Mr. Gentry said.

"As long as it's G-rated," Will interjected.

Mr. Gentry and Samantha both made a face at him.

Will lifted a hand in self-defense. "Just thought I'd point that out," he said dryly.

"It probably should be kind of written in code," Samantha agreed. "So your wife knows it's for her?"

She asked questions. Mr. Gentry answered. Fifteen minutes later, she had what she thought was the final draft of the ad.

She handed it over for the two men to peruse.

*WANTED: Second chance for lovesick male. Step by step reunion okay. If interested, call 555-3148.*

"Looks good to me," Mr. Gentry said.

Will nodded his approval. "Me, too."

"You're going to have to let her know it's running," Samantha warned, "Or this could be a disaster. When does the next edition of the newspaper come out?"

"Early tomorrow afternoon." Mr. Gentry looked at his watch. "I think I've got just enough time to take it over."

"Keep us posted," Samantha urged.

"I will." Mr. Gentry waved as he set off.

"And don't give up the faith," Will called after him. He turned to Samantha, looked at her intently before curving his lips in a half smile. "Some women are worth fighting for."

"What's that supposed to mean?" she asked as soon as Mr. Gentry was out of earshot.

"You know what it means," Will retorted.

That was the problem. She was pretty sure she did. Pretty sure Will McCabe was not about to stop hitting on her. Even more certain that if he kept up his pursuit, she just might find herself surrendering…to more kisses and caresses….

A fact he intuited well.

Will leaned on the porch railing close to her. "Just as you know that if you were to stay in Laramie and start your own firm here, you'd have clients of all types and budgets lining up at your door."

Samantha finished her cold drink and squeezed the can in

her hand. "Which might or might not make me popular around here."

"What do you mean?"

Using both hands, she crumpled the can even more. "If I had my own firm, I wouldn't take every request. I'd have to believe in the product and think I could benefit the person wanting to hire me." Deciding the shady porch was a little too cozy for comfort, she went in search of the recycling bin, in the garage.

Will followed her and tossed his can in. "Can you do that now?"

"Not as a junior account exec at a big firm." Samantha walked back in from the garage, through the kitchen. Deciding that space was too intimate, she went out on the back veranda and stepped down into the yard. She prowled the flower beds, looking for weeds to pull. "When I was at Gallimore, Smith & Tomberlin I had to work on a few real stinkers."

Will settled on the steps, watching. "The worst being?"

Finally locating a weed, Samantha reached over to yank it out. "An herbal supplement that claimed to help people lose weight." She stood there, remembering. "There was no proof that it did any such thing, but there was a lot of money behind it. The company wanted an extensive magazine and mail order campaign. We were told to use testimonials the company provided, and let's just say it was pretty clear a lot of the before and after photos had been artificially altered in a way that was just not believable."

Will rested his arms on his knees. "But you had to do it anyway."

Samantha's lips twisted in disgust. "They were paying the agency five million dollars. I had no choice, even though I felt I needed a shower to wash off the sleaze every time I worked on it." She tossed the weed aside and went to sit down beside him. "If I had my own company, I'd have the luxury of picking and choosing my clients."

He turned his head toward her. "And the downside?"

Samantha sighed. "It would be a struggle to get it off the ground, financially, and I'm not sure I want to live with that kind of uncertainty."

"You could get a start-up loan," Will suggested.

Samantha knew just who he had in mind. "From Howard or one of his investment-banker friends?" she guessed bitterly. "Forget it."

"There's always the Small Business Administration."

"That takes time. There's a lot of red tape. I need income now."

He smiled. "At least you're thinking about your options."

*In more ways than one,* Samantha admitted ruefully to herself. "I better get in the shower." *Before I'm tempted to sit here with you any longer.* She formed her lips in an approximation of an enthusiastic smile. "I have a bachelorette party to attend."

SAMANTHA STOOD on the front porch of the McCabe home, waiting for the limousine to pick her up, wishing tonight were like any other evening, yet knowing it wasn't.

"Do you know where you're heading?" Will asked, seeming to sense instinctively that something was going on with her. Again.

Ignoring the close scrutiny of those blue eyes, Samantha smiled. "Yes. I do." Unfortunately. She'd had all day to wonder if she was going to handle it fine…or flip out.

Will sauntered closer, inundating her with the scents of spicy cologne, soap…and man. "How come the guys can't know?" he murmured huskily.

Pretending she didn't want to grab on to him and never let go, she replied, "Because Molly doesn't want any of the groomsmen to get the bright idea of crashing our party."

Will twined his fingers through hers and flashed a wicked

smile that made her think he wanted to kiss her again. "I wouldn't crash it."

Samantha wished he would. She'd like nothing better than to be rescued from this evening's event—and whisked away to safety—by him. But it wasn't going to happen. She'd been running so long now. Like it or not, she couldn't run forever. She had to do this. Had to at least try and move forward with her life. Coming to Laramie, spending time with Will McCabe, had shown her that.

Seeing the white stretch limo round the corner, she withdrew her hand from Will's and moved numbly toward the steps.

"At least give me a clue," he insisted, trailing after her.

If only she could unburden herself that way. "Talk to Howard."

Will paused at the catch in her voice. "Do you think he knows?"

Aware that the April evening was already taking on a distinct chill, Samantha took her cardigan and slipped it around her shoulders. She couldn't believe she'd been talked into wearing a frilly debutante sundress and heels. But then, that was what all the women were wearing tonight. "From what I've seen, Molly tells him everything."

Will held her eyes, still looking like he wanted to rescue her. The surprise was, she wanted it, too.

The vehicle was filled with laughter when Samantha climbed in. There were eight other women inside and, she was told, three other stretch limos were headed toward the lake. The bride-to-be looked especially radiant.

Samantha was happy for Molly, even as she wished the party was going to be held anywhere else.

"You have to know," Will said to Howard, when he reached the Laramie Lake Lodge, where the bachelor party was being held.

Howard removed the cigar from his mouth, ready, it seemed, to take the secret to his grave. "The question is, why do *you* need to know?"

Because Samantha had seemed nervous. And she never got nervous.

Will lit his own cigar. "Just curious," he fibbed, not ready to admit how much Samantha was beginning to mean to him.

Howard cast a look over his shoulder at the men gathering around the bar. He drew Will out onto the deck overlooking the water. "You promise you won't tell anyone else?"

Will nodded.

"Molly rented the *Liberty,* a party boat, for the evening."

Will stared at his friend in disbelief, every protective instinct rushing to the fore. "You put your sister on a dinner cruise— after what happened?"

Howard's face hardened, reminding Will that Samantha's brother never talked about the way their parents had died, or the impact it'd had on him, either. "How did you know the specifics?" he demanded.

"That's not important. The point is Samantha shouldn't be on a boat."

Looking as stubborn in his own way as Samantha often did, Howard muttered, "The accident happened a long time ago."

Will thought about the way Samantha cried in her sleep. "It's still fresh to her," he stated roughly.

"I've been on plenty of ships with no ill effect."

"Of course you have. You were in the U.S. Navy. You signed up for that. Has Samantha even been on a boat since it happened?"

Finally, Howard began to look as worried as Will felt. "I assume she has."

"But you don't know for sure," he snapped.

His friend gestured helplessly. "How could I? She won't talk to me!" Howard moved closer. "The question is, why are you so concerned?"

*Because I care about her, maybe more than I even knew,* Will thought. "She looked jittery as hell when she left tonight."

Now, at last, Will knew why.

"Nothing is going to happen on the lake."

That, Will thought, was not the point.

"And even if it did, Samantha is a world-class swimmer now. I made sure of that."

Again, beside the point, Will thought impatiently. "Does Molly know how traumatized Samantha was by what happened?"

Howard turned away, lost in his own memories. "Molly and I've never talked about that day."

"Well, maybe you should," Will countered. "And with more than just your wife-to-be."

# Chapter Nine

"Feeling any better?" Molly asked, an hour and a half later.

"I'm certain the Dramamine will kick in soon," Samantha assured the guest of honor cavalierly. She drew in a deep breath and kept her eyes on the sun lowering slowly in the western sky.

"I wish I'd known you were prone to seasickness." Her lips pressed together in a moue of regret, Molly sat down beside Samantha.

It wasn't the motion of the boat on the water, Samantha thought in mounting despair. She could barely feel the party boat gliding across the smooth surface of Lake Laramie. It was just being on the water that was causing the sick, shaky feeling deep inside her, making her feel that the evening—which had just gotten started—would never end. Why had she ever thought she could handle this? Samantha wondered, blotting the perspiration from her temple, the back of her neck.

"I'll be fine." She hoped. "I just need to sit here quietly and get a little air."

Lewis McCabe's wife, Lexie, joined them on the deck outside the stateroom. Unlike Molly, Lexie was focused on the horizon. She shaded her eyes with her palm and frowned. "That speedboat seems as if it's coming right at us."

Samantha's stomach took another precarious dip. Aware

she was on the verge of becoming completely hysterical, she clenched her hands in her lap. How had the evening gone from barely manageable to out of control?

The captain came out to join them. To Samantha's relief, he didn't seem at all upset. "We've got a guest coming aboard," he announced pleasantly.

Molly's brow furrowed as the craft came to a stop by the boat's ladder. "But everyone's already here," she protested.

"Not quite," the captain corrected with an enigmatic smile. Through the swarm of pretty women at the railing, a male silhouette appeared.

Samantha caught her breath at the sight of the handsome man strolling straight toward her. "What is Will McCabe doing here?" Lexie asked, perplexed.

Conversation ground to a halt. Like a mythic warrior emerging just in the nick of time, Will made his way through the additional guests pouring out of the main salon, not stopping until he reached the bench where Samantha was sitting. His gaze met hers.

"Aren't you at the wrong party?" Molly teased.

Will's eyes crinkled at the corners. He smiled like an unrepentant sinner. Unable to tear her gaze away, Samantha flushed self-consciously.

"I didn't think Samantha's sweater would keep her warm enough, once the sun goes down and the wind kicks up," Will fibbed with a choirboy earnestness no one in their right mind would have believed. "So I brought her a jacket from the gift shop to wear, too." He produced a hooded pink-and-white windbreaker with Lake Laramie Lodge written on the front. He winked flirtatiously at Samantha and sat so close to her that their bodies were touching. Ignoring the lacy white cardigan she already had tied around her shoulders, he patted her knee companionably and pressed the nylon jacket into her hands. "I didn't want you to get too cold."

Samantha didn't know what Will McCabe was up to now. She only knew that, with his razor sharp powers of observation, he was the last person she wanted to see. "And if you ladies believe that, he has some oil rights to sell you," she quipped.

Chuckles abounded. "Ah. Isn't that cute."

"They're sparring."

"He must really be into her."

"Or something," Samantha agreed with a self-deprecating smile.

Will shrugged off her cynical attitude. Although she had been perspiring just moments before, the warmth of his solid frame was surprisingly welcome. He winked at the women gathered around them, stretched his long legs out in front of him and continued making a mockery of Texas chivalry. "Just doing my duty as the best man, seeing to the continuing comfort of Molly's maid of honor."

"Nosing in where you don't belong, you mean," Samantha muttered beneath her breath.

"You've certainly brought some color back into her face!" Molly declared.

"She was feeling a little under the weather until you arrived," Lexie agreed.

Ignoring her stubborn resistance, Will wrapped an arm about Samantha's shoulders. "All the more reason she needs a jacket to cuddle up in." He smiled wickedly. "Or me."

"Oh, please!" she declared, waving off the amused approval of the group. They all thought he was here to hit on her. Samantha knew his motive was something deeper, and far more dangerous to her peace of mind. "You're not here to bring me a jacket. Nice at it is," she added guiltily, too inherently polite not to acknowledge a gift, however untoward.

"You're crashing our party!" someone else accused.

Will waggled his brows at the growing crowd of females around him. "You think?"

Recognizing the change in vibes between Will and Samantha, Molly tilted her head. "What was wrong with the bachelor party?" she asked curiously.

Again, that hapless shrug and smoldering smile. Will kicked back even more, purposefully crowding Samantha. "The way I see it, I can smoke cigars and play poker anytime. I figured there would be more excitement and better company here. Looks like I was right." He regarded the cluster of pretty sundresses and prettier women around him with unabashed admiration. "You ladies do look spectacular tonight."

Samantha rolled her eyes. "You are so full of it," she muttered in a low voice.

His breath warming the shell of her ear, he whispered back, "Full of admiration for you, you mean." He slid his palm across her shoulder, down her arm.

"Maybe we should give the two lovebirds a moment alone."

"I wouldn't go so far as to call us that," Samantha said brusquely.

"I would," Will replied.

Soft laughter surrounded them.

"If only all our men were that romantic," someone said wistfully.

"I think they are…."

The voices faded as the women moved away.

The scent of the lake teased Samantha's nose. The fading sun flooded them with shimmering light. With Will by her side, she realized, she felt safe in a way she hadn't since her parents died, years before. The knowledge both comforted and annoyed her. As much as she wanted to lean on him, she also knew she was leaving in a few days to go back to New York. "So what are you really doing here?" she asked, determined to keep the protective barricade around her heart.

Will ripped the tags off the jacket. Hands on her shoulders, he urged her forward and slipped it around her. "I always wondered what goes on at a bachelorette party."

She eyed him skeptically. "You're telling me you've never crashed one before? Never charged after a damsel you perceive to be in…need of a warmer wrap?"

"This is a first. For both."

The sincerity in his blue eyes had her heart hammering in her chest. So why now? Why her?

Samantha decided she wasn't quite ready to discover the answers to those questions, for fear of what they would reveal about his intentions toward her.

He inspected her more closely. "So what generally goes on at these things?"

Glad to have the conversation on more neutral ground, Samantha leered at him comically. "Depends on the bachelorettes. For instance, if you were hoping to see women do Jell-O shots, strip off their bras and swing them around their heads, while dancing on the bar, you're at the wrong party."

He apparently already knew that and had come, anyway. Chuckling, he asked, "Ever been to a party like that?"

"What do you think?"

He studied her. She had the feeling he'd just pictured her naked. The surprise was, she was thinking of him that way, too. And liking it.

"No," he said finally.

She struggled to get the frog out of her throat. "Right again."

"How come?"

Samantha pleated the fabric of her skirt between her fingertips. She knew what he was thinking. She'd been to college, where opportunities to behave like a total idiot were plentiful. "Drinking to the point of recklessness has never really been my thing." She already had enough regret in her life; she didn't need any more. "I like being in control."

"Yeah." Will reached over to take her hand in his, stilling

the restless motion. "I don't drink anymore, either." He caught her speculative look, continued frankly, "I had a problem in high school, after my mom died. That's how Kate—my stepmom—got to know our family. She recognized the problems my dad was too grief-stricken at the time to see, and made us all deal with them."

The parallel stung. "Like you're trying to do with me?" Samantha said quietly.

Will leveled his gaze on her. He gave her that you-can-lie-to-yourself-but-you-can't-lie-to-me look. "Pretending a hurt doesn't exist doesn't make it go away. Kate made us see that, hard as it is, you've got to suck it up and deal rather than run away."

Before Samantha could think of a smart-aleck comment to deflect that razor sharp observation, the captain strode past. Once again, guests flooded out of the main cabin. "Will McCabe, look what you started!" Susie Carrigan chided.

Samantha turned her gaze in the direction everyone else was looking and saw the party boat was getting close to shore again. On the docks stood some thirty men. Many of whom, Samantha swiftly figured out, were either married to or dating the women at the party.

"If he gets to crash your party, so do we!" Howard exclaimed, leading the charge onto the party boat's main deck. Howard wrapped Molly in his arms and gave her a joyful kiss that soon had everyone clapping and whistling. "Now it's a party!" he said.

As other equally affectionate greetings followed and the party took on a completely different tone, Howard released his hold on Molly and came over to join them. He knelt in front of Samantha, the mea culpa she had always wanted to see on his face. "I'm sorry," he said quietly. "I didn't think."

Hot tears gathered in her eyes at the unexpected compassion in her brother's low voice—compassion she would have given anything to hear during the ten long years when she'd been stuck in foster care.

Anger and guilt coalesced inside her. Her only escape was the tough-as-nails attitude she had perfected in her youth. "It's really not your problem," she said.

"YOU NEED TO GIVE YOUR brother a chance to make things right," Will said several hours later, when they arrived back at the house.

Deciding those McCabe-blue eyes of his were much too perceptive, Samantha adapted an airy stance as she stripped off the jacket he had brought her, and dropped it on a living room chair. She was too confused to have this conversation. "And you need to stop sounding like a broken record."

"Your brother was wrong to put you on a boat tonight without first checking to see how you felt about being back on the water."

Too restless and overwrought to go upstairs to bed, but not in the mood to talk, she opened up the armoire and sat down in front of the television. She picked up the remote and switched it on.

Will took the device from her and turned off the TV.

Ignoring her sigh of displeasure, he pushed the ottoman in front of her and sat down, so close their knees were touching.

She glared at him and pulled her legs back a half inch. "Just so you know, I'm all talked out."

He hunched forward, elbows propped on his thighs, further invading her space. "Just so you know, I'm not."

"I thought that was a woman's line."

He ignored her sarcasm. "You're not getting out of this."

"We'll see about that."

They stared at each other in silence. It didn't take her long to realize his resolve was every bit as strong as her own. That didn't mean he was going to win. "I don't care how long you want to sit there, staring at me. We're not having any kind of heartfelt discussion this evening."

"It's time you started dealing with the accident, Samantha."

The little knowledge Will displayed about her parents' death hit her hard. Suddenly, it was difficult to think straight, even harder to marshal her defenses. She slouched back in her chair and finally muttered, "What did Howard tell you about that?"

"Nothing." Will shrugged out of his sport coat, tossed it onto the coffee table. Compassion lit his eyes. "Your brother doesn't talk about the boating accident that claimed your parents' lives any more than you do."

Amazed that that would be something she and Howard had in common, Samantha felt her heart constrict. "Then how do you know how our parents died?"

"The online archives of the *Beaumont Daily Register*."

Shivering the same way she had when she'd hit the murky waters of the lake, Samantha pushed away the memory of that awful day. She shoved herself off the sofa, tripping over his legs and the ottoman in the process. "Damn you."

He caught her hips to steady her. She shoved his hands away and stalked toward the stairs. "I do not need your help."

He followed her deliberately. Catching her arm, he swung her around to face him. "I think you do. I think you're tired of shouldering your pain alone."

True, but there was no way she was going to admit it. "You really need to mind your own business."

He grasped her shoulders so she couldn't cut and run. "And you really need to start talking about the tragedy and what it did to you before you implode."

Samantha had heard this plea before, many times, many ways. She dredged up an old excuse. "I don't have any memory of what happened."

He narrowed his gaze, allowing, "Maybe you didn't, right after it happened. But somewhere along the way that changed. And you just haven't told anyone."

Samantha knotted her fists at her sides, furious that he had seen through her carefully constructed facade. "What would it matter, even if I did?" she said.

His attitude remained as implacable as a stone wall, yet his tone was gentle. "It helps to talk about things."

Hot, bitter tears pushed at the back of her eyes. Regret choked her throat. "Maybe some people. Not me."

He gave a scoffing sound that made her want to hit him. "Have you ever tried?"

She grabbed hold of the newel post and pushed past him. "I talked to a lot of psychologists when I was in school. I always told them the same thing. Which happens to be exactly what I've been telling you. The past is over. I've dealt with it and moved on. I'm not going back there." *Not in my head. Not in my heart.*

"Except you do go back there," he argued, just as passionately. "Every night in your sleep. You shake and cry and probably relive the whole damn thing!"

Suddenly, Samantha couldn't hold it in anymore. She gave him a punishing look. "You want to know what happened?" she cried angrily, tears spilling down her face. "I'll tell you!" Maybe then— when he knew every ugly detail—he would leave her alone.

Will took her hand, tried to guide her back to the living room. She shook him off and sat down on the stairs instead, resting her elbows on her knees and burying her face in her hands. She could feel him hovering next to her, patiently waiting. She couldn't bear to look in his eyes. Lifting her head, she stared at the ornate front door instead and began to speak in a voice hoarse with pain. "My parents had a twelve-foot fishing boat they liked to take out on the lake near our home. It was my dad's pride and joy. Every Sunday afternoon that the weather was good we went out in it. Sometimes he and my brother fished, other times he just drove it around the lake. We always had life vests with us, but my mom and dad found them to be bulky and uncomfortable and never wore theirs."

She hitched in a breath, ashamed that even after all this time she could barely hold it together, just thinking about what had happened. Which was why when Will sat down beside her on the stairs, and put a comforting arm around her, she didn't protest. "As my brother got older, he didn't want to wear his life vest, either. Because Howard was eighteen, they didn't make him. But I wasn't that strong a swimmer at that point in my life," Samantha said, her voice breaking audibly in the harsh silence, "so I had to wear mine." Tears burned her eyes, raced down her cheeks. Samantha swallowed hard, regret and self-loathing threatening to overwhelm her. "I didn't like being the only one with a bulky life vest on. I thought it made me look like a baby, and I used to complain about the straps constantly. To appease me that day, my mother loosened them so they weren't bothering me."

He saw where this was going; Samantha could see it in his eyes.

Trying not to think how he would look at her after this was over, she shoved a hand through her hair. "It was such a beautiful September afternoon." Fresh tears misted her eyes, blurring her vision. She had to force herself to go on. "I can still remember being out on the lake that day, enjoying the warmth of the sun and the wind in my hair."

It was the last completely happy moment she'd ever had.

She turned her head to look into Will's eyes. "My dad had stopped the boat, so he and my brother could drop a line. I was sitting on the edge, against the rail, reading a book. My mom was in one of the captain's chairs at the front, doing the same."

Memories came, as fast and destructive as the actual event. Samantha's chest tightened to the point she could barely breathe. "And that's when the two speedboats came out of nowhere."

She shook her head, stunned to this day by the unexpectedness of it all, how the joy had turned to terror. "They must have been racing, they came upon us so hard and so fast." She shuddered, able to see it now every bit as clearly as she had then.

"The wake of the first craft splashed up into our boat, drenching us all. The amount of water alone probably would have sunk us," Samantha recounted, her stomach churning.

Will tightened his grip on her. Needing him as she had never needed anyone before, she leaned into his comforting warmth. "There was no way we could have bailed enough of the water out in time. Not that we had the opportunity to try."

She shook her head as angry, anguished tears slid down her face, unchecked. With a shaking hand, she brushed them from her face. "The wake of the second vessel rocked us so hard it flipped us over."

She shook her head, crying even harder. "I don't think I made a sound. There was just this tremendous whoosh and my feet went out from under me. The book flew out of my hands and then I was completely underwater, caught up in the choppy waves." She saw it as she had then, in terrifying slow-motion.

Will brought her closer still.

"I remember being disoriented at first, scared by the blackness of the water so far down, then panicking, trying to move, to swim, whatever it took to get some air. It didn't help that I'd slipped out of my life jacket. I thought I was going to die, that I'd never make it to the sunlight.

"Then somebody—maybe it was my dad—pulled me to the surface. I was choking, gasping for air." A dull, shock-laden feeling came over her once again.

"I remember my dad shouting at Howard to swim for the shore. My mother, who was bleeding from her temple, starting to follow my brother. And then she disappeared beneath the surface."

An event Samantha saw over and over in her dreams.

She felt impossibly cold, numb, just as she had then.

"My dad told me to hold on to the hull of the boat—it was upside down in the water—then he left me and dived down after my mom." Samantha turned to look into Will's face, saw his eyes were shining wetly, too. She swallowed, wishing the outcome had been different. But there was no rewriting history, any more than they could change their feelings about the traumatic event.

Keeping one arm laced around her, Will took her hand, squeezed it hard. Samantha welcomed his compassion, his strength.

"That's the last thing I remember until I woke up in the hospital, and some social worker came in to tell me that my parents had both drowned trying to save me, but that Howard was okay." She sighed tremulously, burying her face in her hands once again. Then she pushed to her feet and paced away. "And Howard blames me for the loss of our parents to this day."

IT TOOK A MOMENT for what she'd said to sink in. Will studied the agonized expression on her face. "Where did you get that idea?"

Samantha brought her crossed arms in close to her body. Shuddering as if standing in the bitter cold, she cupped a hand beneath each elbow. "It's why he put me up for adoption and joined the navy. He wanted to be too far away to have to deal with me." She trembled harder.

Will wasn't sure whether the sound that escaped her was a pent-up sob or a bitter laugh.

The look she gave him was troubled. "Because he knew that if I'd been wearing my life vest the way I was supposed to, I wouldn't have slipped out of it," she explained, more distraught than ever.

She sniffed. "I wouldn't have nearly drowned, and my dad would have been able to tend to my mother instead of wasting precious time saving me."

Will looked around until he found a box of tissues. He brought her a fistful and shoved them into her hand. "And maybe your mom would have passed out or become disoriented or suffered a cramp and drowned, anyway," he told her gruffly, wrapping his arms around her again. He rubbed his palm up and down her back while she leaned against his chest. "Maybe your dad still would have died trying to save her."

Samantha drew in another halting breath, flattened her hands against his chest, then stepped back slightly. "The point is we will never know." She paused to blow her nose. "And Howard will never forgive me."

Knowing her brother wasn't the one who couldn't forgive Samantha for what she had and hadn't done, Will strolled away from her and perched on the arm of a chair. "You're preaching to the choir," he said quietly. "I know all about self-recrimination and regret."

"How?" There was a wealth of pain in that single word.

Will couldn't stand the raw vulnerability in her gaze. "Because I suffered plenty of it after my mom died," he told her honestly, knowing what it was like to hate your own weakness and push everyone else away. "I beat myself up for all the missed opportunities to be close to her before we knew she had cancer. And for all the things I couldn't bring myself to say after we found out, for fear it would sound like I thought she was going to die and that would somehow jinx her recovery."

He shook his head, aware his eyes were welling up as badly as Samantha's now. "I thought my mom wanted me to be strong 'cause I was the oldest. I thought I was supposed to set this tough-guy example for my younger brothers. And instead all I did was forfeit my last chance to be with her, to let her know how much I loved her," Will said thickly. "And then she was gone, and there was no way to go back and fix it, or give us a different outcome than the one we got."

Samantha came closer. "I'm sure your mother knew how much you cared about her," she countered gently.

"The point is," Will stated in a choked voice, "I had a chance to say goodbye to her and I blew it. I ran scared from her illness whenever it got too much for me to handle, and that seemed to happen nearly every day. And for a long time after she died, I couldn't forgive myself, any more than you can forgive yourself for the mistakes you made."

Samantha's chin quivered. She empathized with him—but only to a point. "Look, I'm doing what I need to do to set things right as much as they can ever be." She put her hands up as if to call a halt to further soul-searching. "I'm participating in Howard's wedding, just like he asked, and then I'm going to walk away and let him and Molly live happily ever after."

It wasn't that simple. Will sensed Samantha knew it, too, even if she wasn't quite ready to admit it. "What about you?"

She lifted her shoulders in an indolent shrug, replying even more irritably, "I can take care of myself."

"Can you?" He wasn't about to let her get away with that. "Is that why you were on the verge of panic tonight, just being on a boat?" he challenged. "Why you continue to have those nightmares?"

She tried to slip from his grip. He brought her closer instead, determined to make her accept the truth. "Those nightmares are about the accident, aren't they?" he demanded as their chests collided.

"Why does any of this matter to you?" Samantha cried.

"Because," Will said gruffly, "*you* matter to me."

# *Chapter Ten*

Samantha barely had time to react before his head was lowering toward hers. His lips fastened over hers, and just that suddenly, all her pent-up emotions came tumbling out. Anger and confusion fled, replaced by the here and now of his riveting, passionate kiss. She moaned softly as he clasped her to him and deepened the kiss until it was so wild and reckless it stole her breath. Unable to turn away from such raw, aching need, such undeniable gentleness and yearning, she kissed him back with the same lack of restraint.

This was the way she had always wanted to be kissed but never had been. He kissed her as if he meant to erase every hurt she had ever suffered.

Samantha melted against Will in boneless pleasure, savoring the feel of his firm chest against her breasts, the safety of being cradled in his strong arms. When lower still, his hardness pressed against her, passion swept through her, weakening her knees. For too long she had kept her need for closeness, for enjoying the physical side of life, at bay. No more, Samantha thought. For who knew what tomorrow—even tonight—would bring?

He slid his hands down her arms, his palms erotically caressing her bare skin, his lips pressing delicious kisses to her throat. "I want to take you to bed."

She trembled all the harder. Looking into his eyes, she decided to let down her guard and be honest. She offered a crooked grin. "For once we're on the exact same page."

His mouth took on a mischievous slant. "About damn time," he said. Tucking an arm beneath her knees, he carried her up the stairs and down the hall, to the bedroom he had inhabited in his youth. Her heart raced as he set her down beside the bed. His eyes were dark with desire as he lowered her dress to her waist, dispensed with her lacy bra. And then his lips were on her flesh, sending her into a frenzy of wanting. She whimpered as he cupped her breast, caressed the taut, aching tip, and then covered her lips again in another searing kiss. Her fingers fell to the waistband of his slacks, but he was dropping to his knees, taking her dress all the way off. Sandals and panties followed suit.

"Beautiful," he murmured, caressing the flatness of her abdomen, the tops of her thighs. Hitching in a breath, she caught his head in her hands, slid her fingers through his hair.

He touched and kissed her, until sensation layered over sensation in a wave of pleasure that was almost her undoing. "Oh, Will," she whispered, as desire detonated inside her. She came apart in his hands, trembling and gasping. He held her until the aftershocks had passed, and then lowered her gently to his bed.

Samantha watched him undress, taking his time about it, looking his fill all the while. "Seems I'm not the only one who's beautiful here," she teased as he stretched out beside her on the twin bed. He was all warm, satin skin and taut muscle, rock hard. The obvious depth of his desire for her gave her the confidence to be aggressive in going after what she wanted, too, and before long she rolled him onto his back and moved on top of him. Draping her body over his, she caught his head between her hands and began to kiss him, languidly at first, then with increasing ardor, driving him to the brink even as the ridge of his arousal grew ever harder.

Liking the fact that he was willing to let her set the pace, she slid ever lower, kissing and caressing, exploring as she went, not stopping until his body was throbbing every bit as much as hers.

And then they changed places yet again. Will parted her thighs with his knee and rose above her, taking possession of her in the most intimate of ways. She arched against him, gasping as he surged into her slick, wet heat. Wanting, needing, she moaned as he entered and withdrew in slow, shallow strokes, their mouths mating every bit as intensely as the rest of their bodies. Until there was no more delaying. Nothing but passion as he took everything she offered and gave her everything in return.

Samantha hadn't known she could want a man like this. Hadn't known she could meet as an equal. Hadn't guessed she could feel as if she belonged in someone's arms this way. But she did, she discovered, as Will pressed into her as deeply as he could go, and the two of them experienced the ultimate pleasure and release. And came slowly, slowly back to reality.

With it came the horrible panic that had haunted her for years.

Realizing the enormity of what they had just done, Samantha caught her breath and tried to escape.

Will shifted his weight to one side, but refused to let her go. "Tell me what you're thinking," he urged.

Her emotions in turmoil, Samantha said, "You don't want to know."

"Yes. I do."

Her chest rose as she took a long, unsteady breath. "Okay then. This was a mistake." A big one.

He didn't look as ticked off as she would have expected. "Because…?"

Because it left her feeling more vulnerable than ever. And vulnerable was the last thing she wanted to feel while still trying to sort out her feelings about Howard, returning to Texas, and being here with Will.

"What we just shared wasn't...real," she said raggedly.

"Funny, it felt real enough to me." He ran a hand down her thigh. "And I'm sure we could make it feel that way to you if we tried again."

No kidding. Six seconds of contact and she was ready for blastoff once more. Determined to get out of this predicament with her pride intact, Samantha plucked his hand from her skin. "This was just a fling," she explained patiently. *An infatuation.* "Time apart from the reality of our lives." And oh, what a time-out it had been.

He wasn't buying her abrupt reversal. "The only mistake you've made is pushing people away."

Samantha sat up, dragging the sheet with her. "Listen to me, Will. I know your intentions are honorable, but I can't do this. I can't get close to you. I can't get close to anyone."

"Yes. You can," Will countered, compassion shimmering in his blue eyes.

WILL KNEW SAMANTHA was right about one thing—they had entered into their lovemaking on a whim, albeit a highly emotional one. But now that the heat and wonder of the moment had passed, he had only to look in her eyes, to see the way she trembled at his slightest touch, to realize what they had done. They hadn't just made love to each other or found solace in each other's bodies. They had forged a connection, found the kind of intimacy they both sought. Even if Samantha wasn't ready to admit it just yet.

"And I'll prove it to you," he promised, loving the way she looked—so beautiful, so ravished. Delighting in the sweet womanly fragrance of her, he took her in his arms once again, knowing that coming together with her like this was everything he had ever imagined it could be.

"Right here, right now," he said, before he slowly, deliberately, lowered his mouth to hers.

He knew she didn't mean to kiss him back, any more than she had meant to kiss him earlier this evening, and somehow that made the culmination of their passion all the hotter. Groaning, he deepened the kiss, testing the silky heat of her mouth and the soft give of her lips against his. She responded just as hungrily as before, wrapping her arms around him, crushing her breasts to his chest. Determined to make her see what they could have if she would just let all her reservations go, Will plundered her mouth with his tongue. As he had hoped, in no time at all she was kissing him back fiercely.

The softness of her body molded to his. With hunger flowing through him in waves, he swept his hand down her body, charting her dips and curves. Able to feel how much Samantha wanted and needed him, he caressed the tender crests of her nipples, then kissed and suckled them until she moaned. Wanting her full surrender, he used a light caress to convince her to part her legs for him once again. Her head fell back as he found the sweet, sensitive spot with the pad of his thumb. To his delight, she sighed in pleasure and closed her eyes. Her breathing grew ragged once more as he continued the intimate stroking, until she was rocking slightly, all fire and passion, leaving no doubt about what she wanted, what they both wanted. Needed. Had to have...

Trembling with a depth of feeling he could no longer deny, watching her face, he slid inside her once again and began to thrust. As he took them to the limit and beyond, he knew in his heart that nothing had ever felt so right.

SAMANTHA AWAKENED FEELING more relaxed than she had in a very long time. Surprised to find herself alone in the single bed, after sleeping wrapped in Will's arms most of the night, she turned onto her side and looked around.

Sunlight washed the gunmetal-gray walls. It didn't appear the spacious room had been changed since Will was a teenager. Posters for rock bands popular way back then lined the wall. An old-fashioned stereo sat atop a tall chest of drawers. Engraved athletic trophies, painstakingly assembled models of military jets, and books filled the shelves. Several photos of a younger Will and a beautiful dark-haired woman—obviously his mother—sat on the table beside the bed. There were more of him and the rest of his family, plus one of Will, Kate and his dad at what appeared to be his graduation ceremony from military training. He looked remarkably happy in all of them. Samantha envied him the completeness of his family. What would it have been like, she wondered, to grow up here, surrounded by people who loved you? Wistfulness swept through her.

The door opened.

Will walked in with a breakfast tray—complete with flowers—in his hands. He looked incredible in a gray U.S. Navy T-shirt and dark blue running shorts. And he smelled even better, like soap and cologne. "You're awake." He settled on the bed next to her.

Samantha sat up and reached for Will's blue dress shirt, slipping it on and tugging it over her thighs. "What time is it? I've got to get over to the Nedermeyers'."

Will looked at her as if she were the most beautiful woman in the world, and he flashed a sexy smile. "It's nearly noon. And don't worry, I saw to Hansel and Gretel. They're fine this morning. Apparently, their jaunt around the neighborhood yesterday calmed them down. No more upset tummies."

"Well, that's good. Thank you for doing that for me."

"Hey, what are friends for?" he said.

Was that what they were now? Friends? And why did she suddenly want to be so much more than that? Why did she suddenly wish she *could* have something long-term with him? Reminding herself she was a very independent person—too independent to get locked into a relationship, long distance or otherwise—Samantha drew a stabilizing breath and swept the hair from her face. She tried for normalcy. "What time did you get up?"

"Around seven," he murmured, looking as if he had been replaying their lovemaking in his mind...and mentally preparing for a repeat performance.

His eyes drifted to the shadowy V between her breasts, making her aware she could have fastened a few buttons on the shirt that she'd borrowed. He leaned forward and settled the tray across her lap. Ignoring the response in her breasts and thighs, she picked up the mug of steaming coffee and lifted it to her lips. "This is like a time warp in here." She said the first thing that came into her mind that didn't involve talking about what had happened in this very bed. What had she been thinking, giving herself over to Mr. Likes to Be in Charge? Who, coincidentally, happened to be not just the best man at Howard and Molly's wedding, but one of her brother's closest friends?

"Yeah." Will looked around fondly, every bit as at home here as he was in his Spartan quarters at the airstrip. "Kate keeps saying she's going to redecorate all our bedrooms—make us clear out all our old stuff so she can turn 'em into proper guest rooms—but she never gets around to it. She's always too busy at the hospital, helping her patients." He plucked a couple of raspberries off the fruit plate he'd prepared, and popped one into his mouth. He pressed the other against Samantha's lips, waiting until she opened her mouth to let him slide it in. "Just between you and me, despite all her proclamations to the contrary, I don't think it's very high on her priority list."

The sweet tang of raspberry melted on her tongue. It had not been her imagination. Will was one very sensual man. So much so that just the memory of last night made her want to be with him all over again. She swallowed around the sudden dryness of her throat. "Why not?"

His eyes gleamed as if he knew exactly what she was contemplating—and was just as ready to go again as she. He picked up another berry and lifted it to her lips. "Well, for starters, Kate isn't into decorating. At all. If the colors match and the furniture is comfortable, she's happy. Second, I think she likes being reminded of how it was when we were all still living at home. She was an only child and always wanted siblings. So then she married into this family that already had five boys, and soon had a baby of her own, a girl. It was quite an adjustment for her."

*As moving back to Texas would be for me,* Samantha thought.

Not that she should even be thinking about it, no matter how hard Molly and Howard were trying to convince her she should.

Samantha slathered butter on her croissant. "I just met Kate briefly, but she seems like the kind of woman who can handle an awful lot. She's so kind and loving."

"She made me understand what a difference having the right person in your life can make." Will looked at Samantha, generating shivers of anticipation deep inside her. "Take you, for instance," he continued playfully. "You look damn fine wearing my shirt."

Samantha quirked her lips, knowing the best way to keep things uncomplicated was to keep the mood light. "Is that a prerequisite for the women in your life?" She nibbled on her croissant. "They have to look good in starched blue cotton?"

"Woman, not women," he corrected in the same husky tone he used when he made love to her. "And yeah—" he held her gaze for a long moment "—an ability to connect with me in bed is one requirement."

Her heart began to pound. Pretending she wasn't thinking about sex, she ate another piece of croissant. "The others?"

He slid his eyes from the hollow of her throat to her lips. "I've got to be able to talk to her."

She told herself she was impervious to his charm. What they were enjoying here was a short-term fling and a lot of flirting. Nothing more. "Doesn't sound too hard, since you're never at a loss for words."

He arched a brow. "And have her understand."

"Also not hard if she has an IQ above, oh…sixty…."

He threw back his head and laughed. "Plus, she's got to laugh at my jokes."

Samantha widened her eyes. "Have you made any so far?"

He grinned. "And she needs to be kind of funny, too."

She eyed him consideringly. "Funny ha-ha, or quirky funny?"

"Either. Both." Will reached out and tugged the end of her hair. "Doesn't really matter, as long as she has gorgeous eyes and hair and a talent for advertising."

She tapped her chin and pretended to think. "I might be able to set you up with a colleague or two of mine."

"I don't do blind dates."

"Ah. But you do go to New York to pick up a woman you've never met before and cart her back to Texas."

He spread his hands wide. "All duties of the best man."

Much more of this sexy banter and she might find herself falling for him—for real. "Was last night part of the chore roster, too?"

"Last night was…" he exhaled, looking conflicted for the first time since entering his bedroom "…something I'd rather your brother not know about. At least not now."

Samantha shared his desire to keep their whatever-this-was-turning-into off-limits. "Ditto that." She sighed, finished the last of the fruit.

"My private life is my own."

"As is mine," she agreed.

Their gazes met. "At last something we agree upon," Will said, his mood turning unexpectedly sober.

In another room, the phone rang. "Be right back."

Will disappeared, and when he came back, he was all-business once again. "We've been summoned," he said.

# Chapter Eleven

"Frankly, I am surprised at you, Will McCabe," Yvonne Gentry scolded, like the former educator she was. She paced back and forth in her cozy living room, which was decorated in floral prints reminiscent of the English countryside. "And you, too, Samantha! How could you have been a party to Oscar's latest bid for my attention, knowing full well how running a personal ad in the Laramie newspaper would embarrass me?"

Samantha put up a hand. "Look, he really wanted to do this, so what could we say?"

"I don't think Mr. Gentry has anything to apologize for," Will said frankly. "He's tried every way he knows how to get back in your good graces and you won't give an inch."

"How do you know?" Mrs. Gentry cried, looking even more upset.

Frustration curled the corners of Will's lips. "I know what I see, and that's a man who is at his wit's end, trying to demonstrate to you that he still loves you more than life."

"Well, if he loves me so much, why is he determined to drive me crazy?" Mrs. Gentry retorted.

"What has he done?" Samantha asked gently, still trying to understand.

"Come and take a look." The older woman led the way into her kitchen, where the butcher block countertops were as neat and tidy as the rest of the house. Samantha saw nothing amiss, but Will did. "Didn't there used to be floral wallpaper in here—sort of like the fabric on the furniture in the living room?"

"Exactly." Mrs. Gentry pursed her lips. "My husband took it down without asking me and painted the kitchen yellow."

"That's a pretty popular color for kitchens right now," Samantha murmured.

"I hate yellow."

"He should have asked you before he did that," Will conceded. "But I'm sure if you asked him to repaper or repaint the room he would do it in an instant."

"Oh, for heaven's sake, Will. It's not just that. Look at this!" Mrs. Gentry swung open the cabinet and pantry doors.

"Everything looks very tidy," Will said.

His former English teacher tapped her foot impatiently. "Notice anything about the cans?"

"They're in alphabetical order, just like the spices?" Samantha noted.

"Exactly. Now who ever heard of putting baked beans next to berry pie filling? Thanks to that man, I can't find anything in my own kitchen. He took everything I use on a daily basis off the kitchen counters, including my stand mixer, which is so heavy I can barely lift it these days. And he didn't stop there. He's gone through every room in the house, reorganizing and repainting and rearranging until I think I'll lose my mind."

"Why didn't you simply tell him you wanted to be in on the decision making process?" Will asked.

Mrs. Gentry scowled. "I did. He won't listen to a word I say. And when he does, he argues with me and tells me everything I want to do is wrong. And then insists on doing it his own way."

"How long has he been like this?" Samantha asked, curious.

"Since we retired from teaching, last June." Mrs. Gentry sat down wearily and buried her face in her hands. "I thought he would get over it, once he got used to being at home full-time. But instead he has only gotten worse."

"Intruding on your turf," Will stated, finally understanding.

"It's to the point where if he moves one more thing, I'm going to scream. So I asked him to leave and go to the fishing cabin."

"Have you been happier since he's been out there?" Samantha asked. She sat down next to her and took her hand.

"No." Mrs. Gentry teared up. "But I can't go back to living the way we have been the last nine or ten months. I just… can't…do it. And since he doesn't get what he has done…" She threw up her hands.

Will sat down on the other side of her. "As much as I sympathize with your frustration, I think you should have tried harder to make your husband listen."

Samantha turned to Will in surprise.

"You're an English teacher," Will continued firmly. "You have no trouble communicating. I know that firsthand, from sitting in your class. You now have a captive audience, a man who is so desperately in love with you he is willing to do anything and everything to get you back. He's ready to listen, Mrs. Gentry. The question is…" Will paused, letting his words sink in "…are you ready to try?"

"YOU WERE A LITTLE ROUGH on her, weren't you?" Samantha asked, during the walk back. "Especially since the ad we couldn't talk Mr. Gentry out of running has really embarrassed her."

Will looked both ways before crossing the street, then waved at a neighbor down the block. "No more than her kicking him out has humiliated him. The way I see it—" he took Samantha's elbow as they stepped over the curb "—Mr. and Mrs. Gentry made a vow to love each other for better or worse, come what may." His lips set stubbornly. "Mr. Gentry is sticking to that promise. Mrs. Gentry is not."

Were they talking about the Gentrys, or Will and his ex? Samantha had a feeling the situation between his former teachers had touched a nerve with him.

"I know they love each other." He paused to get the mail from the box. "You don't walk away from love. It's that simple."

They walked up the porch steps to his childhood home, through the ornate front door. "I had no idea you were so romantic," Samantha teased.

He tossed the mail onto the console table in the hall. "Hey, I'm a romantic guy." Will pulled her into his arms, brushed the hair from her face. Tenderness filled his blue eyes. "Never more so than when I'm around you."

His mouth slanted across hers in a sweet kiss that encouraged her to answer his ardor with her own. He brought her close, wrapping her in his arms. Feelings welled up inside her as she savored the gentle warmth of contact. Her lips parted beneath the pressure of his as his tongue swept her mouth with long, deliberate strokes. She had never felt so safe, so protected, so wanted. Never felt so much passion and need in a single caress.

Samantha was trembling when they drew apart. She had only to look into his eyes to know he wanted to make love again as much as she did. "Oh, Will…." *You're making me want to stay.*

She had the feeling he was going to say something profound, but just then the cell phone in her purse began to ring. Frowning, he stepped back, never having said a word. She retrieved her cell and put it to her ear.

IT DIDN'T TAKE WILL LONG to figure out Samantha was talking to someone from Blount & Levine. "Only one problem," she said, looking stressed again. "I'm not in New York City. I'm in Texas for a wedding this weekend. Sure, you could overnight the employment contract here for signing. I'll give you the address." She read the street address off the stack of mail Will had brought in with them, thanked the caller and cut the connection.

With an uncomfortable look on her face, she explained, "The HR person at Blount & Levine wants me to read, sign and fax a copy of my consent in no later than 5:00 p.m. tomorrow. I'll have to take the originals with me when I report to work on Monday morning." She turned to Will, all-business once again. "Is there a fax machine I could use?"

Was it his imagination or was she starting to look a little bit conflicted about this great opportunity she had? "Kate and my dad have one in the study."

Her shoulders slumped slightly in relief. "Great."

"You don't look happy."

Samantha disagreed. "I'm ecstatic."

"You don't have to take that job," Will insisted. "You have options."

Samantha walked to the study and sat down behind the desk. "Blount & Levine is the only option I want."

"I don't believe that," he told her quietly.

She flipped open the lid of her laptop computer and switched it on. "You just want me to be around long enough to see the ad campaign for McCabe Charter Jet Service through to completion."

Will shrugged. "It's your idea. You should get the credit." He paused, trying not to fantasize about what it would be like to help her form a new dream. One that included Texas, family, and most of all, him. He perched on the edge of the desk. "You could use the work for me to launch your own business here."

Samantha's lips curved in a semblance of a smile. "You're beginning to sound like Molly the mayor."

"Just because someone else suggested it doesn't mean it's a bad idea." Noticing she was ready to get down to work, he stood and prepared to leave. "Think about it," he said over his shoulder. "I could be your first client."

"GOT A MINUTE?" Will asked Molly half an hour later.

She looked up from her desk in the mayor's office. "Come on in."

For privacy's sake, Will shut the door behind him. "I really need to meet with Howard as soon as possible."

Molly put down her pen with a frown. "That's a problem. He went to the East Coast and won't be back until right before the rehearsal dinner tomorrow night."

Will sank down in a chair and propped his elbows on his knees. "I thought Howard had the week off."

Molly's expression turned enigmatic, leaving Will with the impression that she would have liked to reveal more but couldn't. "He had something he needed to take care of before we leave for our honeymoon."

Will's gut told him it had to do with Samantha. She was not one for surprises and would not appreciate one from her brother, especially if it was the sort that interfered in her life. "Does this have anything to do with the job offer Samantha just got from Blount & Levine?"

Molly rocked back in her chair. "Why would you ask that?"

Will shrugged. "Because I know Howard. And I know how he is when he sets his sights on something. Specifically, getting Samantha back to Texas for good."

Molly took off her reading glasses and rubbed the bridge of her nose. "He's trying to put together a deal that may or may not work out, on such short notice." She lifted a hand, palm out. "I'm not at liberty to say more."

Will hoped Howard hadn't gone overboard in his efforts. "Corrupting the job offer she got would be a mistake."

"You don't need to worry about that. He hasn't talked to anyone at Blount & Levine."

So what was Molly hiding? "Howard's not responsible for her getting the opportunity, is he?" Will asked. Samantha would have railed against that.

"No. He doesn't want her working in New York, period, if he can help it."

"So how is Howard planning to keep that from happening?"

Molly bit her lip.

Now Will was certain his friend's trip had something to do with Samantha. A fact that made his request all the more urgent. "Listen, Samantha and Howard need to talk privately, as soon as possible."

Molly gave Will a perceptive look. She had known him long enough to realize when he was withholding pertinent information, too. Will knew he could tell Molly what Samantha had confessed to him regarding her feelings of abandonment and blame, but he didn't want to do that. He wanted Samantha and Howard to come at each other, their emotions raw, defenses down. He didn't want them having a chance to emotionally prepare, strategize or stubbornly dig in, for fear their defenses would keep them from connecting the way they needed to.

"You know something about the reasons behind their ongoing estrangement, don't you? Samantha's confided in you."

Will nodded. "Let's just say I think they have a chance to bury the hatchet, if you and I can get them together for a heart-to-heart without them suspecting what we're up to."

Molly was already on board. "You want do this before the rehearsal dinner or after?"

Will knew the kind of revelations that needed to be made could not be crammed into a finite amount of time, and were likely to be extremely draining and emotional. "After would probably be better," he replied. "They need to open up to each other." He looked Molly in the eye. "The two of us are going to have to join forces to see that they do, even if it means talking all night on the eve of your wedding to Howard."

"I agree. They need to work this out, the sooner the better. You just tell me where and when." Molly promised, "I'll get Howard there."

SAMANTHA HAD JUST finished putting on her running shoes when Will returned to the house, carrying some bags from the hardware and grocery stores. Dark hair rumpled, a quarter inch of beard lining his ruggedly handsome face, he looked ready for anything that came his way. The spring fever she had been fighting off all week came back to hit her full force. Suddenly all she could think about was taking him by the hand and going back to bed with him, to spend the rest of the day making wild, passionate love.

"Going somewhere?" he asked, taking in her cap-sleeved cotton shirt, worn jeans and sneakers.

Samantha turned her glance away from the T-shirt that delineated his wide shoulders and six-pack abs. "I have to take care of the goats," she said, releasing a pent-up breath.

He regarded her smugly, a sense of purpose glittering in his eyes. "Hang on a minute while I put this food away and I'll go with you."

Her heart gave a nervous lurch. "I don't require your help."

Will grinned. "That's what you said yesterday, as I recall, and you ended up sprinting all over the neighborhood."

Samantha made a face, even as she thought about how nice it was to have someone watching over her, and how easily she could get used to such attention and care. "I'm more experienced this time. I won't be letting them out of the pen."

Will continued to regard her skeptically. "I could still help."

She didn't want to think about what could happen between them—what she wanted to happen between them—if only their situation was different and they were both living in the same place. But that wasn't the case, she reminded herself. Will's life would always be here. Her place was in the New

York advertising world. "You did it this morning and I appreciate that, but it's my responsibility."

He gave her a look that said he wasn't pleased she was pushing him away again. She couldn't help it. The more she was with him, the more she wanted to stay in Texas. And it couldn't happen. Surely he had to know that.

He pressed a light kiss on her temple. "Give Hansel and Gretel a hug for me."

Pretending not to be the least bit affected by the gentle caress, Samantha rolled her eyes. "You are so funny."

Will folded his arms in front of him. "Seriously, you better reassure them or they're likely to get the—"

Samantha knew only too well what malady the goats were likely to get and interrupted him. "Goodbye." Then she walked out the door and over to the Nedermeyers, enjoying the April day.

To her relief, Hansel and Gretel seemed fine this afternoon. Cleaning out the pen was relatively easy. Samantha petted them both, then set out their feed and water. Hands in her pockets, she lounged against the inside of the chain-link fence. The two goats kept pausing and sending her funny looks.

"I know I don't have to stay while you eat," she said. "But I'm going to anyway."

They continued to look at her with round eyes. "So I don't want to hurry back to Will," she continued conversationally. "It's not as if we have anything big going on this evening. I plan to do some more work on the copy for his new ad campaign. I have no idea what he is going to do."

Hansel bleated, as if to disagree.

"Okay, so I do have a clue what Will is likely to do." Samantha leaned in close and lowered her voice to a whisper. "I think he's going to try to seduce me again."

Gretel swung her head from side to side.

"I know, I know." Samantha lifted a hand. "I never should have allowed us to…um, you know…in the first place. But I couldn't help it. He is just so sexy, and he made me feel so good. I haven't felt that way in a very long time. But even so…it's not as if it actually meant anything."

Hansel and Gretel both looked skeptical.

"Either you two are understanding every single word I'm saying or I'm projecting my emotions onto you."

Hansel snorted and pawed the ground. Gretel sat down. She looked as emotionally drained as Samantha felt.

"The point is, I'm too wise a woman to get in over my head with a man like Will McCabe."

And Samantha believed it. Until she got back and inhaled the deliciously spicy aromas wafting from the kitchen. She strolled in, hands in her pockets, trying hard not to be impressed by the sight of Will at the stove, stirring four big stock-pots of meaty chili. As abruptly as her spirits had risen, they deflated. "You didn't tell me you were having a party." She had, she realized belatedly, been counting on having him all to herself this evening.

He gave her an innocent look. "I'm not."

"Okay." She wondered if the way to a woman's heart was through her stomach, too. "A little hungry then?" she teased.

Will wielded a can opener like a pro. "Even King Kong couldn't eat all this." He emptied a dozen cans of ranch-style pintos into the simmering concoction.

She edged closer. "Are you really putting beans in that?"

He gave her a two-fingered salute. "Yes, ma'am, I am."

She scoffed. "Texans don't put beans in the bowls of red."

Will picked up a large spoon and dipped it into the chili. "I learned to enjoy it this way when I was in the Navy. Before you know it, I had the rest of my family eating it this way, too." He lifted the spoon, blew on it slightly, then turned his sexy smile on her once again. "Come here a minute and taste this for me." Keeping one hand cupped beneath it, he held the spoon to her lips. "Do you think it's hot enough? I'm thinking it needs to be a lot spicier."

Samantha savored the delicious flavors melting on her tongue. "Maybe a pinch more chili powder," she decided finally.

He also added cumin and Mexican oregano. "Now try."

She savored the new mixture. "Nice and hot."

Will winked. "Just like me."

Feeling that familiar jolt of attraction, Samantha stepped safely back, out of range. "Too hot for your own good, you mean."

He let his gaze scan her lazily, lingering on her breasts and thighs before returning to her eyes. "Does that mean I'm not getting lucky?" he asked.

Samantha declined to answer, pretending she wasn't privately envisioning Will clearing the table with one sweep, and the two of them stretching out over it. Doing her best to be all-business once again, she turned to the kitchen sink. "I'll help you clean up."

"Whoa." He moved swiftly to stop her. "Don't throw those cans away. We have to wash 'em and save 'em."

She handed them over, tingling as their fingers brushed. "Why?"

"We need them for the back of the car." Will put them in the sink for washing. "We have to make the Just Married sign and prepare the cans to tie to the bumper tonight."

Samantha frowned, perplexed. "That's not the job of the maid of honor," she said.

"It is now."

"You're just trying to get out of work."

Will pointed to the poster board and cans of pink and blue paint. "Painting, maybe." He picked up a brush and tossed it to her.

"What's difficult about that?" Samantha asked, settling down in front of the poster board.

He plunged his hands into the sudsy dishwater. "I lack artistic ability."

Picking up a pencil, she began to sketch the outline of the letters freehand. "I can't believe you're that bad."

He turned his head to observe what she was doing. "I got an F in art in high school."

"Maybe for bad behavior," she allowed, noting he really did seem impressed with her skill.

"Seriously, I can't wield a brush with anything resembling accuracy."

Samantha finished *Just* and started in on *Married*. "So use a Magic Marker," she suggested.

"I already bought the paint."

Finished, she put down her pencil. "So take it back and do an exchange."

He looked at her as if he was thinking about kissing her again. "Lost the receipt."

Samantha pretended *she* wasn't thinking about kissing *him*. "They know you," she countered, demonstrating she could be just as stubborn as him. "They'll remember you were just in. Plus," she added, already thinking about whether she wanted to start with blue or pink paint, "it's not like they don't know you around here."

Will sighed. "Too much trouble."

That reasoning she could buy. Prying open the lid, she stirred the paint with the wooden stick the hardware store had provided. "So back to the chili," she continued, wondering what he was really up to here. "Are you having a party this evening—or some other time?"

His grin widened. "Only if you agree to come."

"Not that kind of party," she scolded.

Will finished washing the cans and left them in the drainer

to dry. He wiped his hands with a cotton dish towel. "Too bad. That's the only kind I'm interested in." He ambled over to hang out beside her.

Samantha painted with slow, even strokes. "Then why are you making so much chili?"

Will turned a ladder-back chair around and sank down on it. "Because," he explained, "I needed the cans."

Samantha shook her head in mounting bemusement. "You couldn't have just saved them as you used them?"

"Sure," he allowed with another shrug. "If I'd been thinking about it the last six months. Which I haven't been. It didn't occur to me until this afternoon that I was going to have to 'fix up' the car for them."

Okay, that made sense in a convoluted way. "I gather you've never done this before?"

He shook his head. "Whenever I was best man, I was always able to talk someone else into doing it for me."

No surprise there, either, Samantha thought. Will struck her as the kind of guy who usually got what he wanted out of life.

He went back to stirring the chili. "Come over here and taste this again."

Resisting the opportunity to be that close to him, she kept painting. "You're the chef."

He dipped up another spoonful. "I value your opinion."

She watched him come near. "You're just playing around." But when he lifted the delicious smelling concoction close to her mouth, she couldn't resist taking another small taste.

He watched her expression. "What do you think?"

"Much better," she decided.

He tasted it, too, and frowned. "Still not hot enough."

Walking back to the stove, he added more red pepper and Tabasco before giving the bubbling chili another stir.

Samantha shook her head in exasperation and kept right on painting while Will tasted it again.

"Well?" she asked.

"Pretty good," Will announced finally. He set the spoon down on the ceramic rest in the center of the stove. "I'd actually like it a little hotter, but Kate and my dad probably wouldn't, so I better stop now."

Finished painting, Samantha stood and stretched.

Will nodded at a stack of plastic containers on the counter behind her. "Hand me some of those, would you?"

She knew an excuse to get her near him when she heard one. "You're freezing this?" That at least made sense.

"Yep, in two-serving portions. It'll be my Mother's Day gift to Kate."

"That's awfully thoughtful of you. Practical, too."

He shrugged off her praise. "My motives weren't totally for the benefit of others. This is also going to be our dinner."

She liked the sound of that, too, Samantha thought wistfully. Perhaps too much.

An hour later, Samantha and Will had finished dinner and dishes. They were sitting outside, punching holes in the bottoms of the cans and threading clothesline through them.

Figuring this was as good a time as any to talk business, Samantha said, "About the ad campaign for your company... I have some suggestions who you might hire here in Texas to finish the job I started."

Will suddenly appeared ticked off. "Don't worry about it," he said harshly, refusing to look at her. "I'll find someone."

She finished tying the last length of clothesline and leaned back to examine their handiwork. She gave the string of cans a jerk and was rewarded with a satisfying clatter on the stone patio. She picked them up and put them in the cardboard box Will had brought out to store them in. "I'd like to know it's someone who will follow the idea I came up with, and not just toss it and start all over again."

With calm deliberation, Will put his tools away, closed the

lid on the box and came toward her. "I don't think it's the ad campaign you're going to have trouble leaving," he said softly, meeting her eyes. "I think it's me."

# Chapter Twelve

Samantha drew a stabilizing breath. "Don't be ridiculous." She had expected him to try and get her back between the sheets. However, she hadn't expected him to stir her soul, or intuitively know what drove her.

"We've got something here, Samantha."

She told herself to leave, but couldn't make herself go. "I know. Sex."

He reached over and took her hand in his, resting it against the hard muscles of his thigh. "Sex is good. Heck, sex with you is great. But we've got something more going for us."

She tried not to think how comfortable her hand felt in his. "Such as absolutely nothing in common?" she quipped.

"I beg to differ."

She reached around behind her for the glass of iced tea she'd brought out with her. "Name…ten things." She bet he couldn't do it.

His quiet assurance filled the space between them. "We both like my chili."

Okay, so the meal had been delicious. And he got extra points for both thoughtfulness and initiative. "That's one." She flushed, fighting the warm flutters spreading through her.

A smile crinkled the corners of his eyes. "We both like our professions."

She raked the edge of her teeth across her upper lip. He was better at this hot-pursuit thing than she had imagined. "Two."

He traced the veins on the inside of her wrist. "We both *like* to work."

She withdrew her hand from his, held up three fingers and lifted her glass to her lips.

"We're both good in bed."

She practically spat out her iced tea, then leveled a droll look his way. "Now you're stretching."

He tilted his head to one side, his gaze lingering on her lips. "But you're not denying it."

"What's to deny?" Samantha said softly. "We both obviously think if something is worth doing, it's worth doing well."

"That's five," he decided with a chuckle.

She was not supposed to be helping him here, Samantha reminded herself. "Consider that my only giveaway tonight."

He grinned as if planning to prove her a liar later. "You like your quiet time to think and reflect every day, too."

"True. And you're only at six, and already stalling out. You see?" She set her empty glass aside. "We're not as compatible as you think."

"I'm not finished yet." Will slid a hand beneath her bottom and shifted her onto his lap. "We both love to read mysteries."

She should have known he wouldn't give up. "How do you know that?" she demanded, reminding herself she was not going to let herself fall in love with him, yet suspecting all the while that it was already too late.

"The books in your apartment." Will's dark head dipped toward her, blotting out everything but him. "And the one you brought with you on the plane."

"All right, that's seven." She grasped the front of his shirt, sounding as breathless as if she'd just run a 10k race. "You've still got three more to go."

He pressed one of her hands over his heart until she felt the strong thud against her palm. "Neither of us care much for being on the water."

Her voice took on that embarrassingly husky quality it got whenever he got too near her. "You were in the navy!"

He smiled and brushed the backs of his fingers down her cheek. "Exactly why I don't want to get on a boat again." He gently kissed the side of her neck. "Spent too much time on 'em then."

Aware that his touch was like magic, sending incredible bursts of heat and electricity dancing across her skin, Samantha added, "Two more to go."

The way he looked at her then made her aware that she had been lonely for more than just sex. He combed his fingers through her hair. "We both like your hair that way, all loose and silky and flowing."

Aware that she had never felt more beautiful or vulnerable, she sassed, "How do you know I like it?"

"Because—" he furrowed his brow "—that's the way you're wearing it. If you didn't like it, you'd change it."

"Fine. I'll give you that one. Although," Samantha murmured, settling carefully on his firm thighs, "I'm not sure I should."

Already claiming victory—in his mind, anyway—he sifted his fingers through the hair at the nape of her neck and tilted her face up to his. "And then," he said in a low voice, "There's the most important thing. I don't want you to leave Texas any more than you want to go."

SAMANTHA SHIFTED OFF HIS lap before Will had a chance to kiss her. Reluctantly, he let her go. "Why are you running?"

"I'm not. I just want to go to sleep." Belatedly realizing she would have been wiser to come up with another excuse at eighty-thirty in the evening, she carried the Just Married sign to the garage for storage. Will transported the cardboard box holding the twin ropes of cans.

"Alone?" he asked, after they had settled both on a shelf and turned to face each other once again.

"Of course."

He liked the humor in her voice and the color flowing into her cheeks. "Bull."

She tossed her head as she moved back out of the garage to the house.

"Lovely lie." He liked the way the lights of the kitchen caught the dark cherry hue of her hair. Better yet was the graceful way she moved as her long legs glided across the wood floor and then up the stairs.

"I don't want to make love with you tonight."

He caught up with her in the upstairs hallway. "Then prove it." He caged her against the wall with his arms. "Kiss me."

She stared up at him from beneath a fringe of thick dark lashes. Although they weren't quite touching…yet, he could feel the heat emanating from her slender body. "Why would I do that?"

Deciding this could get interesting, Will replied, "To show me just how uninvolved you are. If you can kiss me for…oh, say five minutes…"

"Three seconds," she allowed, temper shimmering in her pretty brown eyes.

"Okay, thirty." He continued bartering as if it were already a done deal, watching her cheeks turn an even brighter pink. "If you can do that and still walk away, then you'll get no more seductive moves from me tonight or at any other time."

She blinked, looking as if she wanted him to lead her astray, even as she wanted to keep guarding her heart from any damage he might inflict. "This is your way of seducing me?"

He looked at her. "You're telling me it's not working?"

"Just kiss me and be done with it, so we don't have to go through this again," Samantha ordered, looking every bit as excited as he wanted her to be.

"Okay." Having realized how much fun it was to annoy her, Will played around, made a big show of doing absolutely nothing, figuring a healthy dose of anticipation would heighten the impact of their clinch even more.

"What?" Samantha demanded, looking irritated that it was taking him so long to get started.

He could tell by her shallow breathing how aroused she already was. Doing his best to ignore the growing ache in his groin, he flattened his hands on the wall on either side of her and leaned in even closer. "I just want to make sure you're ready."

"Way past ready," she snapped, only realizing the double meaning of her words after she spoke.

Will grinned and offered with mock gallantry, "Okay, but you have to close your eyes."

"Why?" she asked.

"Because when women are serious about a kiss they always close their eyes."

"How do you know that unless… Do you keep your eyes open?"

He grinned.

She propped her hands on her waist. "Now I am really not going to be able to be serious about this."

"Sure you are." He framed her face with his hands, the yearning to have her admit to the feelings evolving between them stronger than ever. "Just focus."

"On what?" she murmured distractedly.

Slowly, deliberately, he lowered his head to hers. "The feel of my lips against yours."

He fused his mouth to hers, knowing she didn't mean to kiss him back any more than she meant to open her lips to the plundering exploration of his tongue. But submit she did, responding with hunger and need, moaning as his fingers slid through her hair.

Her hands came up to clasp his shoulders and her breathing grew ragged. "Will…"

"And then…on my hands slipping under your T-shirt," he whispered, exploring her breasts.

"Not fair," she whispered, already melting.

Their kiss turned soft and sexy.

"What's not fair?" With the ache inside him growing, he stepped between her legs. He finally knew what he had been waiting for: Samantha Holmes. She was the one…the only woman for him. Taking both of her hands in his, he lifted them over her head, pinning them there. Parting her thighs with his knee, he moved closer still.

Her pulse raced at the heat and intimacy of their contact. She surrendered even more fully to his kiss, until her breathing was just as rapid and shallow as his. She turned her head to the side. "You can't kiss me like that and expect…that I'm not going to…"

He kissed his way down her neck, to the U of her collarbone. "Melt?"

She trembled all the harder, revealing everything she felt, everything she wanted to deny, in her dark eyes. "This is just sex."

"Maybe in your mind," he whispered back, taking a sensual tour of her lips once again. Making her see how right they were together. "In my mind, it's a heck of a lot more."

Samantha wished she could disagree. But even as she tried to formulate a defense for that, she knew he was right. She was falling in love with Will McCabe, against every self-protective instinct she had. To the point she never wanted to leave. And she didn't know quite what to do about it except give in to the moment and experience life to the fullest.

Concentrating only on what she felt, needed, had to have, she returned her lips to his. They were hot and sensual, soft and possessive, tempting and giving all at once. Overwhelmed by the taste of him, she ran her hands across his shoulders, across his chest, until her spirits soared. Luxuriating in the feel of him pressed against her, intensifying the liquid desire she felt churning inside, she deepened their kiss even more.

The next thing she knew, their clothes were coming off. Naked, they came together against the wall. Loving the musky scent of him, the reckless womanly way he made her feel, she molded her body to his, kissing him again and again.

With their lips still fused, he lifted her higher. Impatient for more, she moaned softly, the pinnacle of her release catching them both by surprise.

Knowing she needed him now, he moved inside her, taking the tremors to new, more powerful depths. Pleasure spiraled and they lost themselves in each other, knowing how fragile the moment was. Which was why, Samantha figured, no sooner had Will finished than he had her in his bed again. "That was just the warm-up, you know," he whispered in her ear.

She smiled against his lips, unable to think of a better way to forget her worries. "A warm-up, huh?"

"Barely lukewarm," he decreed, finding the sweet spot behind her ear.

She arched against him. "You call that warm?" She gasped when his lips reached her breasts.

"Lukewarm." His mouth closed around the sensitive, straining tip.

She purred as pleasure slid through her like the golden glow of sunlight on an early spring day. Never one for passivity, she let her hands find him, too. First the hard muscles of his chest, then the smooth skin of his pecs, the tight nipples and soft mat of hair.

"Hey," he growled as they began to tussle playfully, "I'm in charge here."

"Wanna bet?" She grinned as her lips found his navel and went lower still. Then she grinned again when some fancy maneuvering had him doing the same thing to her. Together, they found each other with lips and hands and tongues, letting the needs of their bodies supercede caution while the yearning in their hearts took them to yet a higher plane. Until there was no more talking, no more teasing, only hot love and intense feeling. Until there was a joining of their bodies and souls. And she knew he wasn't the only one who didn't want her to go.

Will had captivated her heart.

THE NEXT MORNING, Samantha's employment contract arrived by express mail. Feeling conflicted, she stepped out onto the veranda to sign for it, then sat down in one of the cushioned wicker chairs. The long-suppressed romantic side of her wanted to turn the offer down flat, in favor of a future here in Laramie, while the ever-present practical side told her not to be a fool. Passionate flings were great—at least that was what she had always heard. But they weren't reality. She couldn't base this life-altering decision on the sexual chemistry she had found with Will McCabe. She had to think about what was best for her—financially, professionally. She had to keep further-ing her career, because at the end of the day her work was all she could rely on to keep her warm and safe.

Aware that Will was watching her, she opened the envelope and began to read. Blount & Levine was being extremely generous in the terms they were offering her. It should have been a cinch to sign the legal agreement and fax it back. For reasons she did not want to examine too closely, Samantha couldn't quite do it. Not without thinking about it a little more first. What if she was overlooking something crucial in the legal language? What if she decided three weeks' annual vacation wasn't enough? Or that she needed benefits beyond medical, dental, vision and portable retirement?

Will inched closer. He'd spent the last hour cutting the lawn for his parents. His T-shirt and shorts were damp with sweat. He smelled of fresh-mown grass and man. "Problem?" he asked.

Her heart fluttered at his nearness. "No."

He continued to look at her in his very determined way for a moment, then wiped his face with the hem of his shirt. "You want help working the fax in my father's study?"

Samantha swallowed around the parched feeling in her throat. "No, thanks. I'll do that later." *When doing so won't make me feel like I'm about to make the biggest mistake of my life in leaving you—leaving what we have—behind.* Avoiding the assessing look in his eyes, she tucked the papers back in the thin cardboard envelope for safekeeping. "Right now, I have to get a wedding gift for Molly and Howard."

Will picked up the water bottle he'd left on the porch and drank deeply.

"I suppose you've already gotten them something?" Samantha asked.

He wiped his mouth with the back of his hand. "A free flight with McCabe Charter Jet to the Bahamas and back."

She whistled as he took another long, thirsty gulp. "That's some gift."

Will shrugged and lowered the bottle. "I owe your brother a lot."

She watched him take off his grass-stained shoes and leave them beside the door. "And a wedding present worth thousands of dollars will take care of the debt?"

He held the front door and motioned her inside. "It would just put a dent in it. But that's okay." He followed her in, then headed up the staircase. "I've got all the time in the world to return some of the favors he has done me."

Curious, Samantha tagged along behind. "What has Howard done?"

Will stripped off his T-shirt and socks and dropped them into the hamper. He stepped in front of the sink and picked up a can of shaving cream, catching Samantha's eyes in the mirror. "He helped put together the investment banking deal that got my business off the ground. Referred clients to me. Used my jet service himself. And he didn't just help *me*, Samantha." Will lathered up his face and jaw, burying two days' worth of whiskers in white foam. "Howard's helped countless other Navy guys getting out of the service, who wanted to start their own businesses or pursue a dream. I know you see him as heartless," he continued, carefully shaving his upper lip, "but he's actually a very generous man."

"To everyone but me," she corrected.

Will rinsed his razor, shook off the excess water before employing it again. "You haven't given him a chance."

Samantha leaned against the bathroom door. The intimacy of the moment comforted her as much as it dismayed her. She tensed her jaw defiantly. "How do you know?"

Will rinsed his face and blotted it with a towel. "He told me he offered to pay your college fees. You refused."

Samantha turned her head as he stepped out of his shorts and briefs, and into the glass-walled shower stall. "Too little, too late," she declared.

Will turned on the water and ducked beneath the spray. "You keep telling yourself that and it may well be," he called.

Samantha tried not to stare at his Adonis body through the wet glass. After the way he'd made love to her the past two nights, it proved an impossible task. "I don't need you to preach to me about the value of family," she declared above the sound of the falling water.

Will looked at her. "Well, someone should."

Samantha focused on the steam rising to the ceiling. "You're coming at this from a completely different place," she insisted, wanting him to understand the depth of her resistance. "You grew up surrounded by people who loved you and were there for you."

"Not always." Will soaped himself efficiently. "Not because they didn't want to be." He rinsed off just as quickly and thoroughly. "But because I wouldn't let them."

"After your mother died," Samantha guessed.

Body glistening, Will shut off the water and stepped out onto the rug. "I was hurting so bad. I was in such a dark place emotionally I didn't think anyone would understand." He paused to wrap a towel around his waist, and then came toward her, not stopping until they were mere inches apart. "And to tell you the truth, looking back, I think there was part of me that didn't want them to understand, because I was so involved in the pity party that had become my life." He paused, cupping the side of her face with his palm. "I think you're in the same place, Samantha, and I think it's time you got out."

"Is EVERYTHING OKAY?" Oscar Gentry asked Samantha as she headed out of the jewelry store an hour later, a gift-wrapped silver serving platter in her hand. Samantha noted the long-married couple in front of her looked surprisingly happy, given their recent estrangement.

"You seem upset," Yvonne Gentry added sympathetically.

That was the understatement of the century, Samantha thought. She was so furious with Will for accusing her of having a pity party for herself that she could barely speak. It had been all she could do to get her purse and leave the house without throwing something at his head. And that baffled her, too. She thought she had cured herself of emotional outbursts years ago, preferring to keep all her feelings locked inside. She hadn't had any trouble doing so until Will McCabe had entered her life, challenging her at every turn.

Not wanting to confide that to anyone, however, she murmured, "It's wedding stress, I guess. You know, all the last minute details that need doing."

Mrs. Gentry nodded. "I think it's that way for everyone, dear." She patted Samantha's arm.

"The two of you look incredibly happy," Samantha noted, not really surprised. It had been clear from the start that they loved each other deeply.

"We had a heart-to-heart last evening and decided to reconcile," Mrs. Gentry said with a smile. The two of them clasped hands and held on tight.

"So our wedding anniversary party is on, Sunday evening as previously scheduled. We'd like both you and Will to come," Mr. Gentry told her.

Samantha felt a stab of disappointment. She had quickly become fond of the older couple, as well as many of the other residents of Laramie. And it was more than just the traditional Texas hospitality. There was a genuine warmth and willingness to help each other out here, something that had been sorely lacking in her life. "I'm not sure I can," she admitted reluctantly. "I start a new job in New York Monday morning. But thank you for the invitation." She paused to hug them both. "I'm so glad you worked things out."

Mrs. Gentry winked. "And you will, too, dear, I'm sure of it."

Still marveling over her attachment to this community, Samantha left the historic downtown area and drove over to the Nedermeyer residence. Hansel and Gretel looked happy as could be, too, maybe because they sensed their owners were coming back later that evening. ·

"This is our last time together, kiddos." Samantha sat down on the bench in the corner while they ate. When finished, they wandered over to her. She reached down to stroke their downy-soft fur, able to see now why the Nedermeyers were so attached to the cuddly animals. "I'm going back to the city."

Hansel pawed the ground and Gretel sat back on her haunches.

Guilt flooded Samantha. "Don't look at me like that," she scolded affectionately as each goat let out an anguished bleat. "Just because the two of you have a happy relationship going here doesn't mean I ever could." They looked at her, seeming to understand. Samantha continued, "Not that Will McCabe has come anywhere near proposing to me, anyway. He hasn't even told me he loves me." Her voice dropped to a confiding whisper. "He just makes love to me like he does. But that doesn't mean he and I are compatible in any other way."

For instance, Will had been dead wrong about the pity party thing. And if she was to stay on here—not that she would ever do that, she amended to herself—the handsome pilot would no doubt be wrong about many more things as well.

Realizing she needed to get home to shower and change for the rehearsal dinner, she bade a fond farewell to the goats. The first thing she saw when she walked into the house was the express mail envelope with the contracts tucked inside. Aware that she had just fifteen minutes to get them faxed back to New York or forfeit the only job she had been offered since being fired, Samantha picked up a pen. With a sigh, she signed her name at the bottom and dated the page, then carried it into the study off the foyer.

This was the right thing to do. The only sensible thing, she told herself firmly as she fed the pages to the fax machine and pushed Send. So why didn't it feel that way?

# Chapter Thirteen

"Will tells me you signed an intent-to-work contract with Blount & Levine today," Molly noted with disappointment soon after he and Samantha arrived at the rehearsal dinner.

Samantha nodded. He hadn't said anything to her except "Congratulations on the new job," but she knew he had been hoping she would do otherwise.

"I wish you had talked to me first," Howard lamented, engulfing her in a hug that felt awkward and comfortingly familiar, all at once.

The more she was around her brother, the more Samantha remembered the happier times before the accident.

Times she hadn't thought about for years.

It made the loss they had suffered—at Howard's behest—all the more daunting. So many lost years, so many missed opportunities to be close. And now he wanted to be family again. She wished she could trust his newfound brotherly devotion. Trust *him*. Being back in Texas brought up all sorts of feelings. She loved the friendly people of her native state, the down-home give-and-take of neighbor helping neighbor. She had enjoyed helping out the Gentrys, bartering with Will for room and board, and even taking care of the goats for the Nedermeyers while they were out of town. How crazy was that? She liked driving the car her brother had provided for her. Enjoyed experiencing spring in the Southwest once again. Enjoyed wearing jeans and boots and Western-cut shirts and even frilly, going-to-church dresses like the one she had on now.

What had happened to the sophisticated East Coast woman who had flown down here on a private jet? Why did all that sleek black in her wardrobe suddenly seem a little gloomy, rather than stylish?

And most daunting of all, why did the thought of leaving Will—and Molly and Howard—suddenly bring a lump to Samantha's throat and have tears burning behind her eyes?

"It's her decision where and for whom she wants to work." Will slid a proprietary arm around Samantha's waist.

Molly flashed an uneasy smile, but to smooth the tension, said diplomatically, "We had just hoped it would be here."

So had Will, Samantha knew. A fact that made his positive attitude all the more admirable and hard to take. If he was as interested in her as he pretended, why wasn't he doing more to convince her to stay? To start her own business here? Was it really going to be as easy for him to let her go as it appeared? If so, did that put him in the same league as her brother, who had walked away from her all too easily years before, after their parents' death? Samantha hated to think she might have put her trust and faith in someone else who was only going to let her down when push came to shove.

Will looked toward the door. "I think the minister and his wife just arrived."

Molly and Howard went to greet them.

"Thanks for the save," Samantha told Will. Taking a deep breath, she pushed her emotional reactions aside. Will had a mature acceptance of their dual careers and lives. She needed to respect and appreciate that, not let it make her feel insecure.

He gave her waist another squeeze and then stepped back a discreet distance. "You're welcome."

"You've been awfully circumspect tonight," she murmured.

Will tucked a loose strand of hair behind her ear. "That's because I'm going to miss seeing you every day."

That confession she hadn't expected. A flicker of hope rose within her, but she quashed it. Of course he was going to miss the hot sex and teasing repartee. She would, too. But her past had taught her that a romantic relationship without love ended up hurting her more than being alone did. It wasn't a mistake she intended to make again. "You'll get over it."

He gave her a long, assessing look, as calm as she was jittery. "I don't want to get over you any more than I think you want to get over me," he told her with resolve. The possessive look in his eyes—the one he always had before he made love to her—deepened. He rubbed his thumb across her lower lip. "But now isn't the time to discuss this."

She managed a smile, too confused by all that had happened to think of a clever response. "You're right about that," she murmured, wishing she was better at showing him just how unaffected she was by their impetuous wedding-week fling.

Fortunately for Samantha, the social demands of the event prevented any further private conversation between herself and Will.

She still didn't know what she was going to do when they returned to the McCabe house later that evening. Were they going to make love? Should she? She knew what Will wanted. Every time he looked at her or spoke to her he telegraphed his intent. Physically, there was no question what she wanted, either. It was the emotional side of her she was worried about, the part that didn't want to leave.

Too soon, Howard and Molly were passing out gift-wrapped boxes to the members of the wedding party—engraved flasks and cigar cases for the men, earrings and necklaces for the women.

"Ready to go?" Will asked as the evening drew to an end.

Samantha nodded, then set about saying goodbye and gathering up her things. By the time they reached his pickup truck, the bride and groom were heading out, too.

"I invited Molly and Howard over for a few minutes," Will told her as he pulled out onto the street.

Something was up. Samantha could tell by the slightly evasive look in his eyes and the cool male determination in his voice. Dread pooled in the pit of her stomach. "I'm tired," she protested.

Will kept his eyes on the road. "It won't take long."

Breaking her heart never had.

Reassuring herself that there was nothing her brother could say or do to make her feel any worse than she already had as a kid, Samantha said nothing more. Obviously, Will's first allegiance was not to her; it was to Howard. What Howard wanted and needed. How ironic was that? She had fallen in love with a man who cared more about her brother than he did about her.

The tense silence between her and Will continued as they got out of the truck and headed toward the house. Howard and Molly were right behind them. Never one for idle chitchat, Will ushered everyone into the study.

"I have something else I want to give you," Howard said to Samantha, as soon as all four of them were settled. He brought out a long slender box the size of a business envelope and handed it to her.

Curious, Samantha untied the bow, opened it the box and felt her jaw drop. She stared at the figure written on the check bearing her name. She knew her investment-banker brother had earned himself a small fortune. Still… "You're giving me a quarter of a million dollars." She felt numb.

"To start your own business here," Howard explained, a ridiculous amount of hope in his eyes. "That's where I've been the past few days. I had to sell off some assets. And I wanted to put together a list of potential clients for you. Friends and associates of mine who would be interested in hiring you."

"It doesn't have to be here in Laramie," Molly interjected swiftly, sensing Samantha's unease at receiving such a lavish gift. "Howard and I know you might be more comfortable in the city. So if you'd like to settle in Dallas or Houston or San Antonio, we can help you with that, too."

Feeling shaken to the core, Samantha closed the lid on the box. She looked at Will. "Did you know about this?"

He shrugged, no expression readily identifiable on his handsome face. "I suspected."

Samantha shot to her feet. A sob shook her chest. Eyes locked with Will, she glared at him a long moment before turning her wrath on Howard. "I hate to break it to you," she told him bitterly, "but you can't buy my love. Even if you did coerce my participation in this wedding."

Howard stood, too. "How about your forgiveness, then?"

Samantha's heart hardened as she thought about what a good guardian Howard might have been, back then, if only he had been unselfish enough to take her in. "Also not for sale."

Her brother rubbed his temples, exhaled, looking weary but not defeated. "Then what is it going to take to get you to forgive me for Mom and Dad's death?" he asked, his voice breaking.

Samantha blinked, not sure she'd heard right. "You didn't have anything to do with that."

Abruptly, Howard's turned white, then a blustery red. He shook his head, exclaiming in a curt tone, "If I hadn't started swimming for shore—"

*As he'd been told to do.*

Frown lines bracketed his mouth. "—I would have known Mom was in trouble." Tears glimmered in his eyes. He continued in a hoarse voice laced with regret. "I could have helped Dad try to save Mom. At the very least kept watch over you, Samantha."

The realization that he had haunting memories, too, shook her to the core.

"By the time I heard your cries for help, realized what was happening and swam back to the scene," Howard confessed,

"I couldn't find either of them beneath the water—it was too dark and too deep. All I could do was swim to you and keep you aloft until help arrived."

Samantha sank down onto the sofa, the horror of that day coming back full force. She buried her face in her hands. "I don't remember any of that," she said dully.

Howard sat down beside her. He put his arm around her, just as he had that day. "You were in shock by then. When you finally came out of it—at the hospital—you had no recollection of what had happened."

But she remembered what had occurred afterward, all too well. "And you still left me," she cried, pushing him and any comfort he offered aside. "You put me in foster care and just walked away."

"Do you think I wanted to do that?" he demanded. "Damn it, Samantha, I begged them to let me take care of you! But social services wouldn't hear of it. They said you were so traumatized that you needed more help than someone my age could ever give you." Howard shoved his hands through his hair. "And the sad thing is, they were right. Both of us were in pretty bad shape, emotionally. I did all I could do to get through each day myself. I was in no state to be able to help you through your post-traumatic stress disorder and grief. And then you got worse and were so angry…and I blamed myself for that, too."

Their gazes met briefly before Howard continued speaking. "I wrote you letters, but your foster mother at the time read them, and thought they would make an already bad situation worse. She and the social worker assigned to your case told me the best thing I could do for you was stay away, because every time I called, or even sent you a postcard, you were angry and incorrigible for days after. So because I wanted you to recover, I did what they asked— I left well enough alone. Figuring when you were older, when you had recovered from the trauma and grief, we'd be close again."

"Only I couldn't forgive you," Samantha mumbled.

"And I could hardly blame you for that, either," Howard said, just as miserably. "I had mucked things up so badly."

"Oh, Howard. Don't you get it? All I wanted was you." Samantha wiped her streaming eyes. "You were all the family I had, my only link to Mom and Dad. I cried for you every night. I even ran away to try and find you."

Howard nodded grimly. "The social worker told me. I felt responsible for that, too. Everyone involved with your case said your only hope of starting a new life was if you believed the old one was truly over. They felt you needed to be adopted to move on. And so they convinced me to sign those papers. But I only did it on one condition—that I be able to keep tabs on your progress from afar. So every month until you were eighteen, I got a report on you. I saw how good you were doing in school. I found out where you wanted to go to college."

Samantha recalled too well the offer of assistance that had come from him, way too late. "But you didn't have to pay for that. Because I got a scholarship," she said defiantly.

Howard blanched.

Molly turned to him. "If you're going to do this, Howard, you have to tell Samantha the whole truth. You two have to stop holding back."

He swore beneath his breath.

"What aren't you telling her?" Will demanded.

Howard looked at Samantha and admitted sheepishly, "Your full ride was courtesy of me. I had been saving all along, even when I was still in the service, to be able to put you through college. So when I found out where you wanted to go, I met with the financial aid people at the university and explained the situation. They agreed to let me provide for you, but only if I set up a scholarship that kept on after you left. So I did. I wanted you near me. I was living and working in New York

City back then, too. I thought—hoped—the two of us would finally become family again."

Samantha gazed at him, amazed by what he was saying, and dismayed by her own behavior. "But I wouldn't have anything to do with you."

"So I let you go—again—figuring maybe that was best." Howard cast a loving look at his bride-to-be. "Until Molly convinced me otherwise. I love you, Samantha. I have always loved you, from the time Mom and Dad brought you home from the hospital. I'm so sorry I let you down."

Samantha spoke around the lump in her throat. "I let you down, too."

Tears streaming down his face, Howard took her into his arms for a fierce, familial hug. "Let's make a pact. Let's not waste any more time."

Samantha savored the reconciliation that had been so long in coming. "I'm all for that."

"How are you feeling?" Will asked an hour later, from the door leading out to the veranda.

So mixed up she didn't even know how to start sorting out her feelings. Samantha sat on the porch swing, looking out at the backyard. The night was starlit and quiet. A three-quarter moon shone down, and the scent of honeysuckle perfumed the spring air. "Truthfully? I don't know. There's so much to take in." She turned to Will. "All those years. So much wasted time, wasted energy. I resented Howard so deeply." Heartache and uncertainty gripped her once more.

Will sank down on the swing beside her. He wrapped his arm around her, pulled her close and looked her over as if he loved every inch of her, flaws and all. "There's no doubt you both went through hell." He stroked the curve of her shoulder. "But you know the truth now. You've reconciled with Howard. You have a chance to make a fresh start with your brother and your life. The question is, where are you going to do it?"

And wasn't that the fifty million dollar question. Samantha swallowed, wishing her life were as simple as she wanted it to be.

"You have years to catch up on," Will continued.

And so much lingering fear and uncertainty to overcome. Emotions in a tangle, she searched for the first excuse available. "He's going to be newly married."

"So?" Will tossed her a self-assured glance. "Molly has room for you in her life, too. I'm sure she wants to know everything about you."

And she wasn't the only one, Samantha mused. "I don't want to intrude on their first days together as man and wife," she countered.

Will's frown deepened, even as compassion and empathy glimmered in his eyes. "Right."

Samantha's temper flared at the exasperation in his voice. "What is that supposed to mean?"

He got up from the swing, his mouth tightening. "You've already had enough truth for one day," he said. "Maybe we should just call it a night and go to bed. Talk again in the morning."

Nerves jangling, Samantha left the swing and crossed to his side. If he was going to break up with her, now that the wedding week was almost over and she was leaving the state again, she wished he would hurry up and do it. "You started this conversation," she stated stubbornly. "You have to finish it."

He leaned a shoulder against the post of the wraparound veranda. "Is that so?"

She tapped her foot on the painted wood floor. "Yes."

"Okay, you want to know what I think?" he retorted. "I think you're scared to try to be family to Howard again, and let him be a brother to you. Scared it won't work out the way it would have if your parents were still alive. Scared you'll want too much, begin to need him, and then he'll go off and have kids of his own with Molly, and not be available to you…and you'll be devastated once again."

The accuracy of his assessment, coupled with his gentle demeanor, made her catch her breath. Samantha knew how much Will valued family. Almost as much as she feared it. "Molly and Howard have made no secret of wanting to start a family right away. On the honeymoon, maybe."

"Their kids are going to need an aunt."

Reservations built inside her. The tête-à-tête with Howard had been cathartic, but a relationship with her brother and his wife was only a part of what Samantha wanted out of life. "It's more complicated than that," she insisted.

Will smiled, not giving up. "I know you're trying to think so."

Samantha flushed, wishing he didn't have the ability to identify her every vulnerability. "I have a job waiting for me in New York City that took me months to get."

"So?" He came toward her, wrapped both arms around her waist. "Jobs are a dime a dozen, Samantha."

She unexpectedly found herself leaning toward him, finding solace in his strength. "If I turn Blount & Levine down, after having already accepted the position, I'll be burning a bridge."

"And building another."

Samantha drew in a shaky breath, taking comfort in the steady beat of Will's heart.

He stroked a hand over her hair and brushed a kiss across her temple. "You could be happy here in Laramie, Samantha."

Maybe if he loved her as much as she was beginning to love him…

With a determined breath, she stepped back, ready to lay all her worries on the table. "You heard Molly." Perching on the porch railing, Samantha struggled to get a handle on her soaring emotions. "She already suggested I reside in Dallas, Houston or San Antonio."

Will came toward her once again. "Only because you had yet to warm to the idea of setting up shop in Laramie," he stated gently, searching her eyes. "Molly was trying to meet you halfway."

Deep down, Samantha knew that. Deep down, it wasn't really Howard or Molly she was worried about. She curved her hands around the railing. "And what are *you* trying to do, Will McCabe?"

He leaned forward, bracing a hand on the wood on either side of her. "Hold on to you," he murmured, pressing his lips to hers. "Hold on to this."

# Chapter Fourteen

Will knew, even before he captured her lips with his, that he wasn't playing fair. But he had to go against the grain if he was ever going to convince her to stay. And judging by the way she was responding, the way she opened her mouth to his and drew his tongue deep inside, she wanted that, too. Desperate for more, unable to get enough of her, he kissed her with an intensity that took their breath away. Whether she wanted to admit it or not, Samantha had been his since the first time they had made love. He could feel it in the way she clung to him, and the ardent nature of her kiss. And he wanted to be there for her, he thought, as she surrendered to his will and surged against him. He wanted to give her all the love and tenderness that had been lacking in her life for so long.

Sweeping her up in his arms, he carried her up the stairs to his childhood bedroom. To the place he had once sulked in defeat, and now savored absolute victory. The remnants of his past faded away. The only thing that mattered was Samantha, here and now. The joy they found in being together. She felt as strongly about him as he did about her, he knew. He felt her passion and need, tenderness and yearning, in every touch, every caress. Satisfaction unfurled within him.

He let her go long enough to strip down to his skin. Her eyes widened at the sight of his arousal. And then he divested her of her clothing. His hands moved to the back zipper of her full-skirted party dress. Awed by her beauty, he took his time uncovering her supple curves, touching and kissing as he went. And then their lips came together once again. Samantha rose up on tiptoe, wreathed her arms about his neck and kissed him with a hunger and a desperation he not only understood, but felt himself. All layers of restraint fell away. Ever so delicately, he traced her curves. She trembled in response, her flesh swelling to fill his palms. Bending his head, he kissed and caressed her creamy breasts and rosy nipples. His fingers traced from base to tip, then he bent and laved the tight buds with his tongue until her skin was so hot it burned and her hips rose instinctively to meet him. "Oh, Will," she whispered, shuddering all the more, "I want you so much."

"I want you, too." His arms around her, his own body shaking with the effort it took to control his pressing needs, Will drew her down onto the bed. He parted her legs, then touched and rubbed and stroked. She caressed him in turn, exploring his hard ridge with eager fingers.

"Now," she whispered, pushing him onto his back and moving astride him. The V of her thighs cradled his hardness, and he throbbed against her surrendering softness. And when the tip of his manhood pressed against the delicate folds, she moved to accept him.

Will didn't think she could be ready, but she was. The connection turned hot, lusty, reckless. He found her most sensitive spot with the pad of his thumb, easing it back and forth, even as she rocked atop him. He let her take him to new heights, knowing this night, this relationship, was everything he had ever thought or hoped it could be. And then he was going deeper still, harder, slower. Samantha whimpered low in her throat as he filled her to overflowing, until he was embedded in her as far as could be. With neither of them holding back, she climaxed. He followed, fast and fierce. And as they clung together, their bodies burning, their skin damp, Will realized the truth. This wasn't a temporary thing. These feelings he had weren't ever going to go away. And neither, he knew, were hers.

"HOW LONG HAVE YOU BEEN up?" Will's husky voice broke the silence of early morning.

Aware that she had never felt more ecstatic or more crest-fallen in her life, Samantha shrugged. All she had to do was look at his bare chest and low-slung pajama bottoms to recall how he had indulged her with slow deliberate thrusts, until she'd met each one with an abandonment of her own. "Couple hours, maybe."

Will joined her on the porch swing and looked longingly at her mug. She handed it over and he drank deeply of the steaming brew, then grimaced. "I forgot you take cream in your coffee."

She looked into eyes that were dark with passion, glazed with need, and wanted him all over again. Sweetly and softly, hot and fast, it didn't matter. All that mattered was him. What they'd found. What she would soon be leaving behind. She gulped, despite the lump in her throat. Told herself to grow up, accept that this, difficult as it might be, was all a part of life. She smiled weakly. "One of many differences between us."

He kissed the top of her bent, pajama-clad knee. "Come back to bed," he said with a cocky grin. "I'll show you again all the things we have in common."

She shivered, feeling even more overcome by everything that had happened, and what lay ahead.

"Seriously, we've got time before we have to be at the church for the wedding."

Responding to the gentle tug of his hand, she shifted onto his lap. "Most of the day, actually."

"You never answered my question," he said, sliding one arm

around her and threading his other hand through her hair. "What are you doing up so early?" He paused, concern etching his face. "You didn't have another bad dream, did you?"

A tear leaked from the corner of her eye. She discreetly wiped it away with the tip of her finger, but not before he had seen. Aware that he was watching and waiting, she shook her head. "It was actually a good one."

He caressed the side of her face with the pad of his thumb. "Tell me about it."

"It's boring," she whispered.

"You're never boring," he countered.

She swallowed. "You haven't known me long enough." And she hadn't known him. Which was precisely the problem. It was too soon for them to be thinking long-term. Yet that was exactly what she was tempted to do. She loved his take-charge demeanor, the fact that she never knew exactly what he was going to do next. She loved the solid warmth of him, his inherent dependability, his strong sense of responsibility. Will was the kind of man who followed through on any promise he made, simply because it was the right thing to do. The kind of man who could be counted on through thick and thin.

He paused, his glance loving and tender. "All right. Let me guess. You were at the church, ready to walk down the aisle on my arm, and you were naked."

She rolled her eyes. "No."

"Oh, right." He snapped his fingers, teasing her all the more. "That was my dream. And we weren't at the church…we were in my room at the airstrip."

Heat started low in her body and rose to her chest. "Did you really dream that?"

He shook his head, serious now. He kissed her temple. "I don't think I dreamed at all. Didn't need to, since my fantasy woman was right beside me."

At the feel of his lips caressing her skin, Samantha drew

back, aware that the fierce physical attraction between them was part of what was confusing her. "You just can't stop hitting on me, can you?"

"Nope." He flashed a grin. "And you can't stop surrendering to this thing that is bigger than the both of us," he told her huskily.

"Which is maybe why I dreamed I lived in Texas again." *And I was happy. Happier than I've ever been.*

Will regarded her gently. "It doesn't have to be a dream, you know. We can make it a reality for you faster than you can say 'Texas, here I come.'"

Samantha's heart fluttered. "I'd have to find a place to live."

"We could do that together if you want," Will was quick to suggest. "Maybe…" he lifted his shoulder in an offhand shrug "…be roommates."

"Roommates," Samantha repeated, not sure this meant what she wanted it to mean.

"We've been sharing space for the last week and it's worked out pretty good." Samantha ignored the possessive way his hand tightened on hers. "I need to find an actual place to live, too," he continued matter-of-factly. "The room at the airstrip is getting…inconvenient."

Samantha looked at him, wishing she didn't know what an insatiable lover he was. Wishing there was something more underpinning their relationship than friendship and sizzling sex. She swallowed, took a deep enervating breath. "How did you end up living out there, anyway?"

Will's blue eyes took on a serious light. "Cash was really tight when I started the company. I used every investment dollar your brother was able to drum up for me on pilots, planes and hangars. I didn't have much—I had just gotten out of the military—so I started sleeping there. It worked out fine. Until you came along, anyway. Now, well—" he waggled his brows at her "—let's just say you deserve better than a cement-floored room with two twin metal cots."

Samantha tested the waters further. "Suppose I want my own place."

"Then you'll get it," he conceded casually, as if it were an incontrovertible fact. "But I'd rather have you with me."

She stilled. "Won't people talk?"

"That could be a problem." He squeezed her knee, then added persuasively, "But there's an easy way to fix that. Just get married."

"Married!" She could barely catch her breath. "We've known each other a week."

He leaned forward and kissed her throat. "And what a week it's been."

With concentration, she splayed her hands across his chest and managed to drag some oxygen into her lungs. "Will…"

He threaded his hands through her hair. "I don't want to live my life without you, Samantha," he told her.

Her throat caught again. "I don't want to be without you, either," she murmured.

"Then what are we waiting for?" he asked, before he fitted his lips to hers.

WHAT INDEED? she wondered the rest of the morning, and well into the afternoon and evening. A new life beckoned her, Samantha realized as she witnessed Howard and Molly exchange vows and rings. All she had to do was say yes to Will, and by early the next week she'd be saying goodbye to New York City, and living with him in Texas—as man and wife. All she needed was the courage to embrace her love for Will with the same enthusiasm with which she had taken him into her life and her bed.

By the time he disappeared to decorate the limousine that would take the bride and groom away, Samantha had mustered up her bravado and made up her mind. And once she had, she couldn't wait to tell him.

Heart racing, she slipped out of the reception to the parking lot. She found the vintage car Howard and Molly were planning to drive away in—but no sign of Will, no sign of the decorations the two of them had made. Lifting the hem of her bridesmaid dress, so it wouldn't drag on the pavement, she searched for Will's pickup truck. At the same time she spied it, she saw Will and Howard. The two were deep in conversation. As Samantha neared, she picked up strains of what they were saying.

"I'll never be able to repay you," Howard was saying as he handed Will what looked like a check. His back to Samantha, her brother clapped a hand on his friend's shoulder. "When I sent you to New York to bring Samantha back to Texas, by whatever means necessary, I assumed you would figure out a way to goad her into coming. And I hoped you'd use your legendary wit and charm to soften her up, too." Howard shook his head in awe. "But I never imagined you would be able to work the miracle you have with her or get her to open up her heart the way she has."

Nor had Samantha.

"I owe you big, you know that," Will countered gruffly, shrugging off the praise with his customary low-key attitude. "But as far as any more favors go, the way I see it, we're even. Especially since I've gained a lot from this situation, too."

Howard watched him put the check in his inside coat pocket. "What about her staying on in Texas? How's that going?"

Will grimaced, for the first time looking not all that confident. "She hasn't decided, but I've done my level best to convince her."

He sure had, Samantha realized furiously, thinking of how avidly he had seduced her.

"I can't thank you enough for that, either." Howard shook Will's hand.

"Like I said," Will responded, "I've gained from this situation, too."

Distraught, Samantha ducked behind a nearby van so as not to be seen. She waited until Howard was out of sight and Will was tying the cans to the bumper of the departure vehicle, before circling around to his side. He looked pleased to see her. But then, she thought bitterly, he didn't know what she had just overheard. "How's it going?" she asked him as pleasantly as she could.

"Good." He leaned inside the rear of the vehicle to put the Just Married sign in the back window. Emerging, he straightened, flashed her the kind of sexy grin that—until now—had turned her heart inside out. He moved toward her. "It'll be better once I know your answer to the question I asked you this morning."

Samantha made no effort to hide her deep disappointment. "About marrying you—so people won't talk about the proposed living arrangement."

He blinked, taken aback by her obvious hostility. "It wasn't quite as cold-blooded as that."

Resentment stiffened her from head to toe. "Upon reflection, I think it's pretty calculated." And jibed with what she knew about achievement-oriented ex-navy men. "But then, everything about this week has been scripted to achieve a certain result, hasn't it?"

Will grimaced in exasperation. "I don't know what you're talking about, but I have to tell you, I don't like your tone."

She ignored the warning and stomped closer. "And I don't like the fact that my brother asked you to soften me up!"

He blinked. "You heard that?"

"What do you think?" she countered sweetly, not sure whether she wanted to deck him or kick him in the shin.

He thought rapidly. "The conversation wasn't what it seemed."

*Sure it wasn't. And Texas wasn't the Lone Star State.* Samantha propped her hands on her hips. "Did my brother send you to New York City to get me back to Texas by whatever means necessary, and instruct you to soften me up?"

Abruptly, Will looked to be caught in a trap of his own making. "It's not what it sounds like," he repeated.

"I think it is," she argued.

Will's demeanor remained calm, but his voice became a dangerous purr as he looked her right in the eye and stated with devastating clarity, "Then you're mistaken."

Wondering just how much of a fool her soon-to-be-ex-lover thought she was, Samantha leveled an accusing finger at his chest and advanced a step. "Not about the fact that I just saw my brother hand you a check," she stated contemptuously.

Will took the slip of paper from his pocket and handed it over. "He paid the fuel charges for my trip to New York last weekend. I hadn't billed him yet. He wanted to make sure it was taken care of before he left for his honeymoon."

Samantha took it reluctantly. To her confusion, the amount on the check jibed with his story. Stubbornly, she persisted, "I also heard you say the two of you were even now, that you no longer owed Howard anything, nor did he owe you anything."

"That's right," Will confirmed wearily. "My only obligation now is to you."

"And that's ending right here and now," Samantha declared, deciding she had been played for a fool long enough.

A muscle worked in his jaw. "What are you talking about?"

"I came out here to give you my answer." Thankfully, she had witnessed the clandestine meeting before delivering it. "I'm not going to live with you as your roommate or marry you for convenience sake."

Silence fell between them before Will replied, "That's not what I proposed, Samantha, and you know it."

"Yes, it is." Tears of outrage and unbearable hurt blurred her eyes. She lifted her chin a notch and kept her eyes on his. "And that's why I'm going back to New York, because I don't want to be a pawn in this exchange of manly obligations one more second." She whirled away from him.

He clamped his hands on her shoulders and turned her back. "That's not what you're doing." He hauled her into his arms. "You're running again, because you don't have the commitment to be in a relationship with me, or anyone else, for that matter. Whenever the going gets tough, you cut and run."

"That isn't it at all." She wrested herself from his grip. "You betrayed me."

Will released an impatient breath. "I don't deny it started off that way, with me doing everything I could to goad you into staying around long enough to be able to work things out with your brother—which I'd like to point out, you have. But this situation between us soon turned into something else entirely."

He was correct about that. "Something even more foolish," Samantha conceded, charging away from him.

This time he didn't follow. "Where are you going?"

Samantha picked up the skirt of her gown. Her heels clattered across the pavement. "Home to New York City." She turned to glare at him. "And the job that I still have waiting for me."

Will grimaced. "You're making a mistake."

Feeling as if her heart would never be whole again, Samantha said, "The only mistake I ever made was getting involved with you."

# Chapter Fifteen

"What are you two still doing here?" Samantha asked Howard and Molly early the following morning. "I thought you were supposed to leave for your honeymoon first thing this morning."

"The Bahamas can wait," Howard said.

Molly nodded. "We're more concerned about you."

Samantha led the way past her suitcases to the kitchen, where she was still neatening up. "I'm fine."

Howard squinted at her, clearly worried. "You didn't look fine last evening when you left the wedding reception," he pointed out sagely.

"And you weren't the only one," Molly agreed. "Will didn't look so great, either."

Howard glanced around the sunlit space. "Where is he, by the way?"

Samantha focused on lifting the clean glasses out of the dishwasher. "I don't know." She put them away in the cupboard, one by one. "He just told me I could stay here last night without fear of running into him." And to her dismay, she hadn't. Although why she should feel anything but relief about that was a mystery to her. Will had betrayed her. The guilt on his face when she had confronted him proved that he felt so, too. She ought to be glad their brief affair was over, that she hadn't done anything really reckless—like completely rear-range her life to accommodate their newfound passion. She ought to feel happy that she still had a job waiting for her—and an apartment, tiny as it was. Instead, she felt disillusioned and depressed. More than ever before.

Howard lent a hand with the clean coffee mugs. "You're really going back to New York?"

Molly took over the silverware caddy. "We were so sure you were going to change your mind and stay here."

Samantha had been ready to do just that.

"At least," her sister-in-law amended hastily, "before you overheard Howard and Will talking last night."

Samantha had stormed out so quickly the night before, there had been no time to talk about what had happened. She studied Molly now. "Did you know Howard asked Will to do whatever he could to keep me here?"

"Hey." Her brother held up a staying palm. "I never asked him to romance you."

Bitterness welled up inside her. Samantha shook her head in mute remonstration and replied in a hurt voice, "I gathered that was Will's idea." She stacked plates in the cupboard. "Like a fool, I fell for it."

Molly picked up a bottle of spray cleaner and paper towels, and began wiping down the counters. "How do you know his interest wasn't sincere?" she asked.

Howard lifted the plastic sack from the kitchen trash can and tied it shut. "I've known Will for years. He doesn't use people that way."

*That's what I thought, too.* Samantha lined the can with a clean bag.

Howard took the garbage to the garage, then came back in, stepping to the sink to wash his hands. "I don't know why you're so angry at Will and not with me."

Tears blurred Samantha's eyes. She struggled to explain.

"Because now that I know the reasons why you turned me over to foster care, I understand why you were so desperate to set the record straight, help us be a family again."

The corners of his lips slanted downward. "Asking Will to get involved was still underhanded on my part," Howard lamented, his own guilt apparent.

Samantha folded her arms in front of her. "I didn't give you any choice. You had already tried every aboveboard means, to no avail. Even getting me to Laramie for one face-to-face meeting was no easy task."

"Yet Will prevailed where Howard had repeatedly failed," Molly said, pushing Samantha into a kitchen chair. "Do you ever ask yourself why?"

"He was annoying?" she guessed. So annoying, in fact, that cooperating with him had been the only way to shut him up.

Molly shook her head. "There was—is—something about Will McCabe that drew you to him."

"Like a moth to flame, I suppose?" Samantha suggested wryly.

"Like two people who were meant to be together," Molly stated with a stern look.

If that was true, Samantha asked herself, then why hadn't Will said he loved her? Why had he talked about living together, for convenience sake, only bringing up marriage as a necessary device to keep the talk about them at bay? Why had he intimated that his doing that not-so-little favor for Howard had finally evened the score between the two men?

Howard clamped a brotherly hand on her shoulder. "Don't run from him—from whatever it is the two of you have found— the same way you ran from me. Give him a chance before you call it a day. At least try to work things out. And before you do that, ask yourself this. Is it really Will you don't trust? Or just the idea of surrendering your heart to someone?"

WILL WAITED UNTIL NOON before he headed back to the home he had grown up in. As he had suspected, Samantha was long gone, the place in immaculate shape.

He walked around anyway, making sure—or was it hoping? he wondered ruefully—she hadn't left anything behind.

Nothing on the back verandah…just memories of the stolen kisses they had shared. Or in the bedroom and bath she had occupied. Nothing in the study, either, except the advertising campaign she had devised for him.

And would no longer be around to initiate.

Sighing, he sank down behind his father's desk, hearing the front door open and close. He was halfway out of the chair, hope rising in his chest, when he saw who it was—his stepmother and father, back from their respective business trips.

Figuring his dad wouldn't be needing his desk anytime soon, Will sank back down in the swivel chair.

"Don't you look like you just lost your best friend," Sam noted, coming in the door.

Kate nodded, leaning on the arm of the leather sofa. "Thanks for straightening up the house before we got home," she said.

Will couldn't take credit that wasn't due. "Samantha did it."

Kate and Sam exchanged looks that told Will the McCabe family and Laramie grapevines had been working overtime to bring his parents up to speed. "Where is Samantha?" Kate asked casually, the sympathy in her eyes indicating she knew about the disastrous state of his love life. Or now completely defunct love life, he corrected.

Will closed the folder in front of him. "No idea."

Another telltale exchange of looks occurred. "That bad, hmm?" Sam sympathized.

Will put his feet flat on the floor and rocked back in the swivel chair. "What do you mean?"

Kate lifted her shoulder in a delicate shrug, not taking her eyes from his face. "Everyone in town knows the two of you have been staying here together while we were gone, that sparks were flying. To the point Samantha seemed to be considering making Laramie her home from here on out."

Will refused to feel guilty about that, even though he knew that had not been Kate's intention when she'd extended the invitation to Samantha. In his view, it would have been best for both of them had Samantha made her return to Texas permanent. The gossip was another matter entirely, however. "Exactly why I suggested we get married if we did move in together," he stated, in the same practical manner he had made his offer.

Sam's brows took on a disapproving slant. "You asked her to move in before you asked her to marry you?" he asked in astonishment.

Will waved his hand. "I didn't exactly ask her. We were talking about where she might live if she did move to Laramie, and I told her I was tired of bunking at the airstrip, and looking for a place, too. We were already getting along. It made sense for us to share space, divide the costs." At least that was how Will had hoped it sounded. The truth was, he hadn't wanted to be without her. For all the good it had done him. She had cut and run the first chance she'd gotten.

Kate studied him. "I've never known you to be interested in taking on a roommate, no matter how tight your budget was."

"I was doing it to help her out, since she was going to be starting her own business and would be trying to limit her expenses in any way she could."

"Sure you were," Sam noted skeptically.

"I also thought she could use some emotional support." The kind he had been giving her.

Kate switched to counseling mode. "Sounds like she's been dealing with a lot this week," she remarked.

Briefly, Will explained what had transpired between Howard and Samantha since Kate had left for her conference.

"So many wasted years," his stepmom said softly.

Sam reached over and took his wife's hand. "At least Howard and Samantha now know the truth about the events that transpired to separate them in the wake of their parents' death, and have a chance to be brother and sister again. That has to be of great comfort to them both."

Kate tapped her chin pensively. "That doesn't explain why she abruptly walked away from Will, given how close they were growing."

Will related the "favor" he had done for Samantha's brother, the overheard conversation…and Samantha's reaction to it.

Kate shook her head. "There has to be more to cause her to walk away from what could have been a very good life here."

"Haven't you heard? Men aren't the only commitment-phobes."

Kate ignored him. "How much actual courting have you done, Will?"

This was beginning to sound like one of the conversations he and Samantha had had with Mr. and Mrs. Gentry. "None," Will stated flatly, "and for good reason. My relationship with Samantha wasn't like that. It just sort of evolved, from adversaries to friends and confidants to…something more."

Kate scoffed. "I beg to differ. The way you crashed the bachelorette party to take her a jacket, and managed to stay here at the same time she was, all point to your pursuing her in a very traditional man-woman way."

Okay, so maybe he hadn't been all that subtle about his attraction to her, Will thought. "I had no choice but to stay here, since all the hotels were still full and I gave up my quarters at the airstrip to one of the pilots who work for me."

His dad swore softly, unimpressed. "Like you couldn't have bunked in the guest cottage at Brad and Laney's, or arranged for Samantha to do so. Be honest, son. You wanted the proximity." Sam shrugged. "I know how guys think. You wanted to make a major play for Samantha, and time was of the essence, so you made sure opportunity met desire."

Will covered his face with his hand. He was all for his parents treating him like an adult, just not this much of one. "Let's not go there," he groaned, attempting to keep his sex life off-limits for discussion.

Sam continued, "I imagine you were successful in getting and holding Samantha's attention, at least temporarily. But in the end, you didn't sacrifice enough to be with her, and were asking too much of her in return."

Will knew his actions could be interpreted as selfish and self-serving. They hadn't been. And deep in her heart, he figured, Samantha had to know that. "I tried to give her everything that's been lacking in her life for years now," he told his parents in a rusty sounding voice that revealed far more of his emotions than he wished. "Home. Family." Passion...

"What about love?" Kate asked, point-blank.

Will tensed. He hadn't exactly said that. Hadn't felt he needed to. "Words are cheap." He shoved a hand through his hair. "It's actions that count."

"And on that score," his father said derisively, "you really messed up."

Her eyes gentle, Kate agreed. "If a guy proposed to me without mentioning love, I'd run as far and as fast as I could, too. And it wouldn't have taken an overheard and wrongly interpreted conversation to make me sprint for the closest exit. You're not a foolish man, Will. Somewhere deep inside you know this. So why did you propose marriage in a way that gave Samantha no choice but to turn you down? Could it be you have some issues here, too?"

AT SEVEN O'CLOCK Sunday evening, Samantha engulfed Oscar Gentry in a hug. "Congratulations."

"We're so glad you could come," Yvonne said, welcoming her, too. The older couple looked blissfully in love again, as content with their lives as Samantha wished she could be.

She looked around surreptitiously. Although the anniversary party had started over an hour ago at the Wagon Wheel Restaurant, to her disappointment there was no sign of Will. But then, she had expected as much.

As Mrs. Gentry moved to greet the next group of guests, her husband drew Samantha aside. "I need a favor," he said in a low, urgent tone. "I forgot my gift for my wife. It's back at the house. Would you mind going to pick it up for me? It's a small gift-wrapped box hidden behind the Home Sweet Home pillow on the sofa."

"No problem." Samantha smiled.

"You're a lifesaver." Mr. Gentry pressed a key into her hand.

Glad to be away from the romantic aura of the party when she was feeling so completely lovelorn herself, Samantha slipped outside and drove the short distance to the Gentry residence. Soft lights were glowing inside. She unlocked the door, headed in and stopped dead in her tracks at what she saw.

Will stood next to the fireplace with an expectant look on his face. Wearing a starched blue dress shirt and dark gray slacks, he seemed ready for an evening out.

"I take it your being here just now was no accident?" Samantha said lightly.

"Mr. Gentry owed us a favor."

*Us.* She liked the sound of that. It implied maybe the two of them hadn't ended things, after all.

Samantha slipped her hands in the pockets of her sundress and moved closer. Pretending to feel a lot more self-assured than she did, she continued holding his gaze. "Aren't you supposed to be flying Molly and Howard to the Bahamas right about now?"

"Another pilot took over." His blue eyes softening, he closed the distance between them and took her into his arms. "I had important things to do here."

Samantha's heart skipped a beat as he wrapped his arms around her. "Such as?"

Will caught a lock of her hair and tucked it behind her ear, the gesture so tender and gentle it made her want to weep. "First and foremost," he told her huskily, "I had to set the record straight with you."

*Which could mean a lot of things.* "You heard I didn't go back to New York to take that job, after all?"

He searched her eyes. "Why didn't you leave?"

Samantha splayed her hands across his solid chest. "Because Texas is my home, always has been, always will be, and it's way past time I came back," she admitted in a trembling voice, mustering up all the courage she possessed. "And because I'm tired of being afraid. For so long I've lived only in the present. I couldn't deal with the future, when it took everything I had just to get through the day. Saying yes to you, moving in together, planning a life with you, felt like I was tempting fate. I was sure if I let myself love you the way I wanted to, that I would lose you the way I lost my parents and—for a while—my brother. Then we walked away from each other and I realized a life without love is no life at all. And I do love you," she finished softly, tears clouding her eyes as she took the final leap of faith. "You know that, right?"

"I know it." He brought his lips to hers, kissed her deeply. He looked as happy as she felt because there were no more barriers between them. "Just as you know that I love you." He lingered over another sweet, searching kiss. "Not that this was all your fault," he murmured, pausing to look into her eyes. "I bear plenty of responsibility for what happened, too." He took her hand and led her over to a chair. He sank down on the seat, pulling her onto his lap. As she settled comfortably, he stroked his hand through her hair, continued laying bare his soul. "I went into this knowing you resented the heck out of me for goading you to come home to Texas."

The corners of Samantha's lips turned up ruefully. "I know I didn't make it easy on you."

Will shrugged affably. "I expected rejection at every turn."

"But?" Samantha prodded, knowing there was more.

"I had confidence I could win you over in the short term."

"Which you did," Samantha sighed, remembering how passionately they had connected. Not once, but again and again.

Will traced the curve of her mouth with his thumb. "I wasn't sure that I could get you to want to marry me, however, especially in such a short time frame."

That had been a Herculean task, Samantha admitted, given her independent nature.

"So instead of being straight with you and putting my feelings on the line, I hoped to draw you in, bit by bit," Will continued. "I figured it didn't matter why you were with me, as long as you *were*. Now I realize we both deserve better." Sincerity filled his eyes. "You need time to get to know me and my family, as well as yours. Time to settle in, get your new business off the ground. Time to believe what we have is going to last forever."

"I already know that—it's why I'm here. Why I plan to stay." Samantha brought her lips back to his and put her whole heart into the kiss. She tightened her arms around him, knowing all her dreams had come true. "It took my whole life to find you, Will McCabe. I don't want to waste another second."

"And we won't," he promised. At last, she was home to Texas, home to love, home for good.

\* \* \* \* \*

*Look for an all-new miniseries*
*by Cathy Gillen Thacker,*
TEXAS LEGACIES: THE CARRIGANS,
*launching July 2007 with*
*THE RANCHER NEXT DOOR*
*only from Harlequin American Romance!*

Set in darkness beyond the ordinary world.
Passionate tales of life and death.
With characters' lives ruled by laws the everyday world
can't begin to imagine.

# n○cturne

It's time to discover the Raintree trilogy...

New York Times bestselling author
LINDA HOWARD
brings you the dramatic first book
RAINTREE: INFERNO

The Ansara Wizards are rising and the Raintree clan must
rejoin the battle against their foes, testing their powers, relationships and forcing upon them lives they never could have
imagined before...

Turn the page for a sneak preview
of the captivating first book
in the Raintree trilogy,
RAINTREE: INFERNO by LINDA HOWARD
On sale April 2.

Dante Raintree stood with his arms crossed as he watched the woman on the monitor. The image was in black and white to better show details; color distracted the brain. He focused on her hands, watching every move she made, but what struck him most was how uncommonly *still* she was. She didn't fidget or play with her chips, or look around at the other players. She peeked once at her down card, then didn't touch it again, signaling for another hit by tapping a fingernail on the table. Just because she didn't seem to be paying attention to the other players, though, didn't mean she was as unaware as she seemed.

"What's her name?" Dante asked.

"Lorna Clay," replied his chief of security, Al Rayburn.

"At first I thought she was counting, but she doesn't pay enough attention."

"She's paying attention, all right," Dante murmured. "You just don't see her doing it." A card counter had to remember every card played. Supposedly counting cards was impossible with the number of decks used by the casinos, but there were those rare individuals who could calculate the odds even with multiple decks.

"I thought that, too," said Al. "But look at this piece of tape coming up. Someone she knows comes up to her and speaks, she looks around and starts chatting, completely misses the play of the people to her left—and doesn't look around even when the deal comes back to her, just taps that finger. And damn if she didn't win. Again."

Dante watched the tape, rewound it, watched it again. Then he watched it a third time. There had to be something he was missing, because he couldn't pick out a single giveaway.

"If she's cheating," Al said with something like respect, "she's the best I've ever seen."

"What does your gut say?"

Al scratched the side of his jaw, considering. Finally, he said, "If she isn't cheating, she's the luckiest person walking. She wins. Week in, week out, she wins. Never a huge amount, but I ran the numbers and she's into us for about five grand a week. Hell, boss, on her way out of the casino she'll stop by a slot machine, feed a dollar in and walk away with at least fifty. It's never the same machine, either. I've had her watched, I've had her followed, I've even looked for the same faces in the casino every time she's in here, and I can't find a common denominator."

"Is she here now?"

"She came in about half an hour ago. She's playing black-jack, as usual.

"Bring her to my office," Dante said, making a swift decision. "Don't make a scene."

"Got it," said Al, turning on his heel and leaving the security center.

Dante left, too, going up to his office. His face was calm. Normally he would leave it to Al to deal with a cheater, but he was curious. How was she doing it? There were a lot of bad cheaters, a few good ones, and every so often one would come along who was the stuff of which legends were made: the cheater who didn't get caught, even when people were alert and the camera was on him—or, in this case, her.

It was possible to simply be lucky, as most people understood luck. Chance could turn a habitual loser into a big-time winner. Casinos, in fact, thrived on that hope. But luck itself wasn't habitual, and he knew that what passed for luck was often something else: cheating. And there was the other kind of luck, the kind he himself possessed, but it depended not on chance but on who and what he was. He knew it was an innate power and not Dame Fortune's erratic smile. Since power like his was rare, the odds made it likely the woman he'd been watching was merely a very clever cheat.

Her skill could provide her with a very good living, he thought, doing some swift calculations in his head. Five grand a week equaled $260,000 a year, and that was just from his casino. She probably hit them all, careful to keep the numbers relatively low so she stayed under the radar.

He wondered how long she'd been taking him, how long she'd been winning a little here, a little there, before Al noticed.

The curtains were open on the wall-to-wall window in his office, giving the impression, when one first opened the door, of stepping out onto a covered balcony. The glazed window faced west, so he could catch the sunsets. The sun was low now, the sky painted in purple and gold. At his home in the mountains, most of the windows faced east, affording him views of the sunrise. Something in him needed both the greeting and the goodbye of the sun. He'd always been drawn to sunlight, maybe because fire was his element to call, to control.

He checked his internal time: four minutes until sundown. Without checking the sunrise tables every day, he knew exactly when the sun would slide behind the mountains. He didn't own an alarm clock. He didn't need one. He was so acutely attuned to the sun's position that he had only to check within himself to know the time. As for waking at a particular time, he was one of those people who could tell himself to wake at a certain time, and he did. That talent had nothing to do with being

Raintree, so he didn't have to hide it; a lot of perfectly ordinary people had the same ability.

He had other talents and abilities, however, that did require careful shielding. The long days of summer instilled in him an almost sexual high, when he could feel contained power buzzing just beneath his skin. He had to be doubly careful not to cause candles to leap into flame just by his presence, or to start wildfires with a glance in the dry-as-tinder brush. He loved Reno; he didn't want to burn it down. He just felt so damn *alive* with all the sunshine pouring down that he wanted to let the energy pour through him instead of holding it inside.

This must be how his brother Gideon felt while pulling lightning, all that hot power searing through his muscles, his veins. They had this in common, the connection with raw power. All the members of the far-flung Raintree clan had some power, some heightened ability, but only members of the royal family could channel and control the earth's natural energies.

Dante wasn't just of the royal family, he was the Dranir, the leader of the entire clan. "Dranir" was synonymous with king, but the position he held wasn't ceremonial, it was one of sheer power. He was the oldest son of the previous Dranir, but he would have been passed over for the position if he hadn't also inherited the power to hold it.

Behind him came Al's distinctive knock on the door. The outer office was empty, Dante's secretary having gone home hours before. "Come in," he called, not turning from his view of the sunset.

The door opened, and Al said, "Mr. Raintree, this is Lorna Clay."

Dante turned and looked at the woman, all his senses on alert. The first thing he noticed was the vibrant color of her hair, a rich, dark red that encompassed a multitude of shades from copper to burgundy. The warm amber light danced along the iridescent strands, and he felt a hard tug of sheer lust in his gut. Looking at her hair was almost like looking at fire, and he had the same reaction.

The second thing he noticed was that she was spitting mad.

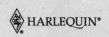

# HARLEQUIN®

## *Mediterranean* NIGHTS™

Tycoon Elias Stamos is launching his newest luxury cruise ship from his home port in Greece. But someone from his past is eager to expose old secrets and to see the Stamos empire crumble.

*Mediterranean Nights*
launches in June 2007 with...

## FROM RUSSIA, WITH LOVE
by *Ingrid Weaver*

Join the guests and crew of *Alexandra's Dream* as they are drawn into a world of glamour, romance and intrigue in this new 12-book series.

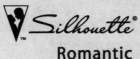

# Silhouette®

## Romantic
# SUSPENSE

**Sparked by Danger,
Fueled by Passion.**

*This month and every month look for
four new heart-racing romances
set against a backdrop of suspense!*

---

**Available in May 2007**

*Safety in Numbers*
(*Wild West Bodyguards miniseries*)
by **Carla Cassidy**

*Jackson's Woman*
by **Maggie Price**

*Shadow Warrior*
(*Night Guardians miniseries*)
by **Linda Conrad**

*One Cool Lawman*
by **Diane Pershing**

---

*Available wherever you buy books!*

# REQUEST YOUR FREE BOOKS!
## 2 FREE NOVELS PLUS 2
# FREE GIFTS!

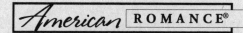

## Heart, Home & Happiness!

**YES!** Please send me 2 FREE Harlequin American Romance® novels and my 2 FREE gifts. After receiving them, if I don't wish to receive any more books, I can return the shipping statement marked "cancel." If I don't cancel, I will receive 4 brand-new novels every month and be billed just $4.24 per book in the U.S., or $4.99 per book in Canada, plus 25¢ shipping and handling per book and applicable taxes, if any*. That's a savings of close to 15% off the cover price! I understand that accepting the 2 free books and gifts places me under no obligation to buy anything. I can always return a shipment and cancel at any time. Even if I never buy another book from Harlequin, the two free books and gifts are mine to keep forever.

154 HDN EEZK   354 HDN EEZV

Name _____ (PLEASE PRINT)

Address _____ Apt. #

City _____ State/Prov. _____ Zip/Postal Code

Signature (if under 18, a parent or guardian must sign)

### Mail to the **Harlequin Reader Service®**:
**IN U.S.A.:** P.O. Box 1867, Buffalo, NY 14240-1867
**IN CANADA:** P.O. Box 609, Fort Erie, Ontario L2A 5X3

Not valid to current Harlequin American Romance subscribers.

**Want to try two free books from another line?
Call 1-800-873-8635 or visit www.morefreebooks.com.**

\* Terms and prices subject to change without notice. NY residents add applicable sales tax. Canadian residents will be charged applicable provincial taxes and GST. This offer is limited to one order per household. All orders subject to approval. Credit or debit balances in a customer's account(s) may be offset by any other outstanding balance owed by or to the customer. Please allow 4 to 6 weeks for delivery.

**Your Privacy:** Harlequin is committed to protecting your privacy. Our Privacy Policy is available online at www.eHarlequin.com or upon request from the Reader Service. From time to time we make our lists of customers available to reputable firms who may have a product or service of interest to you. If you would prefer we not share your name and address, please check here. ☐

HAR07

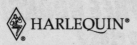

# HARLEQUIN®

# American ROMANCE®

## COMING NEXT MONTH

### #1161 THE MARRYING KIND by Judy Christenberry
*Dallas Duets*
Jonathan Davis was many things—a millionaire, a player, a catch. But he'd never be a husband. For him, "marriage" equaled "mistake." Diane Black was a forever kind of woman, a babies-and-minivan kind of woman. But John was confident he could date her and still avoid that trap. Until he kissed her...

### #1162 THE TEXAS RANGER by Jan Hudson
*Texas Outlaws*
Sam Bass Outlaw knew from the first moment he laid eyes on Skye Walker that he had to get to know her—although the beautiful blonde was hard to get close to, considering the German shepherd, bodyguards and overprotective brother. Whatever Skye's story was, this Texas Ranger would find out!
*Meet the Outlaws—a Texas family dedicated to law enforcement*

### #1163 DADDY PROTECTOR by Jacqueline Diamond
*Fatherhood*
Connie Simmons's neighbor Hale Crandall is wildly attractive, totally irresponsible and doesn't have a serious thought in his head. But after witnessing his heroic rescue of the child she's about to adopt, she realizes she might be wrong. Especially once the unpredictable detective starts to prove he's deadly serious about her!

### #1164 ALEGRA'S HOMECOMING by Mary Anne Wilson
*Shelter Island Stories*
For Alegra Reynolds, returning home means showing everyone how successful she's become. For Joe Lawrence, Shelter Island on Puget Sound is a safe haven for him and his son. Will these opposites learn that home has less to do with the tiny island they were born on and more to do with each other?

### www.eHarlequin.com

HARCNM0407